SALLY JO SURVIVES SIXTH GRADE:
A JOURNAL

Connor,

Enjoy Sally Jo and Eddo's adventures. What are you going to write in your journal?

♡ Karen

SALLY JO SURVIVES SIXTH GRADE:
A JOURNAL

KAREN KELTZ

Happy House Press
Tillamook, OR

Copyright 2012 by Karen Keltz
Published 2013.

Happy House Press
Tillamook, Oregon
www.karenkeltz.com

Printed in the United States of America

ISBN: 978-0985728113
Library of Congress Control Number: 2013948549

PROLOGUE

"Here you go, Sally Jo," my counselor, Ms. Montgomery says to me. She hands me what looks like a book but inside there are only blank pages. "Just for you. It will help, I promise."

I take it and look at the glossy cover which is a picture of water lilies and nothing more, except for the word "Monet" at the bottom. I'm so glad it doesn't say something childish like "My Little Diary" on it. How stupid to put something so inviting on the cover of something you want to be secret. "My Little Diary" just invites nosy people (I'm not mentioning names but someone like Lisa) to want to look inside. And I'm glad it's not all pink. I don't know why all feminine things are always pink because according to my surveys here at school, hardly any girls like that sappy color. How did that "pink is for girls" stuff get started, anyway? Besides, pink doesn't match with my red hair. I like that the cover is mostly green. Green matches.

"The next time you feel like hitting someone, try writing in your journal first," Ms. Montgomery says. She takes my snotty, tear-stained hand in her soft, manicured hands and her voice sounds like a friend's. "Write about what bothers you and take it out on the page instead of another person. Work your problem through at the ends of your fingers, not your fist." Her brown eyes look straight into mine, like I'm an adult, and not a kid of eleven.

Seems to me that's a lot of responsibility for one empty book and a pen. And my angry brain.

I know it wasn't right to kick Roger in the shin when he wouldn't stop picking on that new kid, Melvin Porter, but I also know how it feels to have someone say hurtful words to you. I remember how people picked on my friend Eddo two years ago when he was the new kid. Melvin does look goofy, like a skeleton with skin and big, round glasses, but a good person wouldn't call him goofy-looking and worse to his face.

"Hey, Goofball, did you ride your goofball baby bike to school?" Roger said. "Man, what a doofus!"

Then he pranced around, mimicking riding a tiny bike, letting his tongue loll out and his head roll around all loosey-goosey. Dave and Neal and the other guys laughed, so Roger crossed his eyes and slobbered. Melvin just blushed and looked down at the ground. The more Roger and his friends picked on Melvin, the angrier I got.

The next thing I knew, my foot was whacking into Roger's shin. I know my mouth was talking, too, but I don't remember what it said. It shut up when Roger ran over to the teacher's aide. When she looked up, he began limping like his leg was broken, that faker. She sent me to the principal but he was in a meeting. That's how I got here in Ms. Montgomery's office.

I know I shouldn't go around decking people because they make me angry. My mom has told me enough about proper behavior, but my hands and feet just do what they want sometimes and leave me behind to clean up the mess. Still, nobody but me is going to make me change since I haven't yet and I've been angry since the third grade when people started calling me "Carrot Top" and my dad was killed in a top secret raid in Afghanistan.

"And you know," Miss Montgomery says, bringing me back to this second day of the sixth grade, "you can write about things that are making you happy too, and lovely things, and interesting thoughts you have. If you have doubts, I want you to know that I'm not telling you to do something I don't do. I write in a journal, too."

"You do?" Sometimes people (not naming names, but like my mom, for example) tell you what they think you should do and then they don't do it themselves. "Do as I say, not as I do," they recite when you call them on it. Talk about lame.

"I do," Ms. Montgomery answers. "I want to remember my life and to have something to look back on when I'm older to see what I thought at this age. Maybe I'll marry and have children one day, and they'll be interested to see that their mother was once young with the same concerns they have."

That gets me to thinking. I feel on the brink of something, like this year is going to be important in my life. I don't know what's going to happen every day or week or month, so I will just report after the fact and try to make sense of what happened. I will keep track of all the fun I have with my best friend, Eddo.

Writing should help me know what I think about the stuff that happens to me. Life is kind of like a puzzle and I think we should get smarter figuring out why things happened and why we did what we did.

That's another good reason for writing a journal. I will know what to say to my kids when they have a problem like getting teased for freckles or red hair or whatever. Maybe they won't get in trouble for losing their tempers like I have. I am giving them assignments, too, so they will write their own journals when they read mine.

Ms. Montgomery gets up to go tell her secretary something and leaves me alone for awhile. My eyes look at the peachy-tan wall and Ms. Montgomery's armless chair with rollers on the ends of the legs and I think how we could push each other in races down the hall in chairs like these which is probably why teachers get them and not students. Mainly though, I imagine how I might get married one day and have kids too and then they could see what my life was like way back in 1983–84, in the sixth grade, in Cedar Ridge, Oregon.

When things get so big inside me I can't hold them in any longer, I will write them out. I will start tonight. When they read my journal, my kids are going to feel so lucky. And so will Roger, since I won't be kicking him. Although, he kicked me in the shin in the fourth grade, so I think he had a kick coming.

ENTRY ONE, 9/8/83: MY JOURNAL

This is the first entry of the journal of Sally Jo Benedict—that's me. This is the third day of sixth grade.

I have red hair. People call me "Carrot Top" which I do not find amusing, but rather, stupid. Carrot tops are green and poisonous. People are neither green nor poisonous, at least to my knowledge. Maybe aliens are but I haven't met any yet.

I used to beat the crap out of other kids who called me "Carrot Top." Uncle Jim used to be a boxer and he taught me how to punch so I could do some damage in a fight. I will set aside those skills now, though, because I know people say mean things to make themselves feel better. Ms. Montgomery is teaching me to be more mature.

She says that if people know they can upset you or make you feel bad about something, they will. She is smart about getting along with others and from her I learned that I can choose my response.

For example, I can say, "Too bad you're a cretin." Most kids don't know what a cretin is and while they are standing there trying to figure out whether to be mad, I'll walk away. I can say, "Too bad you're a gelatinous cretin," and they have no idea I have called them a dumb blob. Vocabulary is the ultimate weapon.

Ms. Montgomery told me that instead of worrying about what's wrong with me, I should focus on those things about myself that are nice, like my big brown eyes. Her brown eyes are big, too, and I figure if I grow up to be as pretty and smart as she is then it won't matter if I have red hair. Many actresses have red hair, by the way. Bette Midler, Melissa Gilbert, Ann Margaret. I intend to keep that in mind as well.

I have freckles too. My uncle Jim always teases me and says that I must have stood too close to a pooping cow. I finally discovered what he meant by that and I thought it was disgusting. He used to sing, "She has freckles on her, but she's nice," except he'd put the comma after "but" so it sounded like I had freckles on my BUTT!

My friend Cindy has even more freckles than I do and kids tease her about that. They say things like, "Let's play connect the dots!"

One time she got so desperate that she bought a cream advertised in the back of a comic book. The ad guaranteed she'd get rid of her freckles or her money back but all she got was a huge rash that swelled up her face. She never got any money back either.

She tried buttermilk but she kept it in a dish under her bed so she could put it on in the middle of the night when she woke up. That way her snoopy brothers and sisters wouldn't know what she was doing. It got sour and stunk and her mom made her throw it out.

Another time she tried rubbing lemons all over her face because she read somewhere that lemon juice would make freckles disappear. That didn't work either. She smelled like a sweaty lemonade stand. Her mom tells her that the freckles will go away when she grows up. How can that make her feel any better when she has to live with them right now?

Cindy's freckles don't bother me one bit and they never have, ever since the third grade when I came here and we got to be friends. Maybe we'll just call ourselves The Amazing Freckle Sisters and everyone else will be jealous because they don't have any. I know some people and even some boys don't care if you have freckles because Eddo, who is a boy, is my best friend and that dorky Melvin keeps trying to be romantic with me.

I have started thinking more about other people and the world and stuff since I've been talking to Ms. Montgomery. She just naturally makes a person do that, even my best friend, Eddo. In the next entry I will tell you about how I met him.

Sally Jo's assignment for her future kids who are reading this journal:

What can you do about a part of you that isn't perfect or that people make fun of?

Write down a new and fabulous word you have discovered, like "gelatinous" or "cretin." What does it mean? Use it in a sentence when you are talking to me, your mother.

ENTRY TWO, 9/10/83:
I REMEMBER WHEN

I didn't always like Eddo. I remember when I first saw him in the park, over by the duck pond full of chunky, green algae, the summer before fourth grade, two years ago. My dog, Trixie, and I were sitting on a bench throwing old bread to the ducks when a huge black dog wearing a red collar came running up barking, dragging a short kid at the end of his leash.

Trixie barked back. I don't know what they were saying but it was loud. The ducks all quacked away and people stared our direction.

"Tell your dumb dog to shut up," I said to the kid. He wore black-rimmed glasses that took up his whole face, and a Sherlock Holmes hat. Muddy paw prints covered his blue and white striped tee-shirt.

"His name is Duke. Tell your dog to shut up!"

"Her name is Trixie."

Just then his dog lurched forward, jerking the kid too, and his hat fell over his eyes.

"You shouldn't be walking a dog if you can't control him," I observed, and Trixie and I turned to go. "No use to stay here since the ducks are all scared off by now."

"Oh, go kiss a snake," Eddo spat out.

That made me mad because if there's one thing I absolutely hate, it's snakes.

"The only one I know is you and I wouldn't kiss a four-eyes like you for a hundred-million dollars, Freak Face!"

"Oh, yeah? Well, *your* mother sucks blood, Vampire Breath!"

Trixie growled way deep in her throat. I don't think she liked that comment. Neither did I.

"Then you'd better get your dog out of my way before I FANG you to death, Freak Face!"

"Make me, Carrot Top."

"I don't make trash, I burn it." My friend Cindy taught me this phrase which I was glad about since this was the perfect time to use it. "Besides, your parents already made you and they did a lousy job of it!"

Eddo opened his mouth to say something back to me but whatever he was going to say turned into a screech when Duke took off in a dead run for the duck pond. The leash wrapped around Eddo's arm and the whole thing reminded me of old black and white cowboy movies when the cowboy gets dragged by the runaway horse team. Duke barked, Eddo screeched, and I stared. So did Trixie. She forgot to growl. Her mouth was hanging wide open in astonishment just like mine.

When he hit the water flat on his stomach, Eddo screamed, "I can't swim. Help! I can't swim." His head bobbed in and out of the water and Duke splashed green algae water everywhere so I couldn't tell if Eddo was drowning or not. How could he drown in two feet of water? Nobody else around did anything, probably because they knew the water was only two feet deep or maybe they thought it was just kids playing.

Then I heard a spluttering "Glub, glub, glub," like talk underwater. I did not want to see someone drown before my very eyes, even someone who told me to kiss a snake and who called me Carrot Top.

"Come on, Trixie," I said, and splashed into the pond to help. "Stay!" I said to Duke and looked him right in the face with the evil eye my mother uses when she REALLY MEANS IT. Trixie growled at Duke and he stood still for once, wagging his tail.

I got Eddo around his neck like I learned in the lifesaving course at the Y and I lifted him up so he was standing. I saw that one of the lenses in his glasses had cracked.

He coughed and then he said, "Cripes! You don't have to choke me to death!"

"Did you want to die, you idiot?"

"I wasn't drowning."

"Then what was all that screaming for?"

"I wasn't screaming."

By now, Eddo had made me plenty mad. Not only had he called me names, but he didn't even appreciate my getting soaked up to my knees and saving his life. I dragged him the rest of the way out of the pond, the gunky algae stuff sticking all over our clothes. I prayed there weren't leeches in that pond.

"You're a real creep, you know that? I should sic my dog on you but I don't want to waste my time." I let go of Eddo and he fell down on his face in the muddy, duck-poop grass when he landed. The side with the cracked lens slid to his cheek. I turned to go.

"Wait," he squeaked.

"Now what do you want?" I put my hands on my hips the way my mom does when SHE'S HAD IT.

"I'm sorry," Eddo said.

The more I looked at him, the more I saw he was miserable. What did he expect, anyway? If you can't control your dog, bad stuff is bound to happen.

Duke began licking his face, getting that algae all over his tongue. I didn't see any leeches anywhere.

"I was scared, OK? I hate water. I can't swim."

"Well, you'd better learn. Go take swimming lessons at the Y. Besides, the water in that pond is only two feet deep."

"This has not been a very good day," Eddo said.

"Why not?'

"I just moved here. I miss all my friends. My mom told me to take the dog for a walk and he's gone wild after all those days in the car. I don't even know where I am."

"OK, but you didn't have to be so grouchy."

"I didn't mean all that stuff I said. Duke made me mad, not you."

I looked at Eddo in his muddy, wet tee-shirt and broken glasses, dwarfed beside the enormous, black dog that was now licking the kid's face and I laughed. I don't know why I laughed but Eddo laughed too and we stayed there by the pond laughing until a groundskeeper yelled at us to get away from the pond or he'd call the cops.

"Get the heck out of there, pronto! Can't you kids read that sign? 'No swimming'!" Adults are so dramatic.

"Tell that to Duke," Eddo muttered, and stumbling up the bank, we laughed some more.

As we dried off in the sun, I found out that Eddo had moved from Salem, Oregon to here in Cedar Ridge so his dad could start a new law office.

"I'm nine. How old are you?" I figured he must be about five or six.

"I'm nine, too. I'll be going into the fourth grade. I registered today. Mrs. Woods will be my teacher."

"Mine, too! Now you'll know at least one person in your class. You look short for nine, though."

"Everybody says that." He sighed. "I get so tired of it. It's not like I can do anything to change it. I didn't decide to be short."

"I'm sorry," I said. "People always comment about my freckles and that makes me mad. It really gets my dandruff up."

"Oh, I never even noticed them," Eddo said, squinting through his cracked lens. "Your freckles look fine to me."

"Thanks." I was starting to like Freak Face. "By the way, I'm Sally Jo."

"I'm Eddo, short for Edmund."

"Hi, Eddo."

"Hi, Sally Jo."

Right then I felt like we were friends.

We stared at our dogs for awhile, who panted and sniffed each other. When they lay down, we petted them.

"Kids pick on me because they know they can win," Eddo said. "My mom says that good things come in small packages but that doesn't help much. So every time someone wants to beat me up, I tell jokes. They laugh and forget what they were gonna do. I was gonna tell you a joke until Duke pulled me into the water."

"So I wouldn't hit you?"

"Yeah."

"I won't hit you now since we're partners in crime and all."

"Huh?"

"You know, swimming in the pond. Our big, dastardly deed."

"Oh, yeah."

"Tell me the joke anyway."

"OK. What brand of underwear did the knights in armor wear?"

"I don't know. What?"

"Fruit of aluminum! Get it?"

"With that kind of dorky joke you won't live to be ten. I gotta get home. Wanna come?"

"Sure."

At my house, we tied Duke up outside along with Trixie so they could sniff together.

"Mom, this is Edmund, Eddo for short, and he's going to be in the 4th grade too," I said.

"Very nice to meet you, Edmund, Eddo for short," my mom said, not commenting about his appearance and the algae flaking off on the kitchen floor.

She was baking chocolate chip cookies for some teachers' meeting she had and after we washed our hands, which I thought was a good thing just in case of leeches, she let us lick the bowl and have a couple of cookies.

"Now where do you live, Eddo?" she asked him.

"1030 Cedar Street," he said.

"You live right behind us. We're neighbors!" I said.

"Why don't you walk Eddo home?" Mom suggested, and I did.

On our way to his house, I said, "Do you still think my mom sucks blood?"

"Nah. Chocolate chips, maybe."

We laughed and I thought about Mom leaning down to bite a bag of chocolate chips and saying, "I vant your chips!"

Later, when Mom tucked me into bed, her fluffy, brown hair gathering around her face like little hands when she bent over, she said, "It was nice of you to make friends with Edmund. He's probably lonely here without his old friends."

"He is. That's why his parents got him a dog. Will we ever have to leave this house? A new one wouldn't seem like home anymore."

"It's not likely, Sally Jo. Don't worry about it. Sweet dreams and don't let the bedbugs bite."

It never works when my mom tells me to not worry about something because I do anyway. We'd already had to leave one house behind when we moved here and I didn't want to go through that again.

"I don't have bedbugs," I said, just like every night. Sometimes there are old toenails or sand in my bed but no bugs. My mom says that because her mom used to say it to her.

"Nighty-night," I said, just like I always do.

Now, you may think I'm too old to get tucked into bed but I like it because it's the best time I have with my mother. We talk about serious matters of the day and it's nice to fall asleep knowing someone loves me.

I looked around my bedroom, fixed the way I like it, with the lavender gingham ruffled curtains and my canopy bed with matching spread. I looked at my shelves of stuffed animals, my baseball mitt and my books. My TV on my dresser, next to my cassette tape player and the picture of my dad in his special forces uniform.

I thought about all the memories in my room, the time I had chicken pox, the time I got to have all my friends over for a slumber party, and the day in 1979 in our old house when my mom, crying, knelt at the side of my bed to tell me that my dad had been killed in Afghanistan where he was sent with secret CIA forces.

I hugged Rosco, my teddy bear, who had been with me through all of it from the very beginning. Everything here was a part of me. I knew then how Eddo felt having to leave his old house. We were friends from that day on.

The first time you met your best friend is a good memory to write about.

———————

Sally Jo's assignment for her future kids who are reading this journal:
  Write about something important that happened and start, "I remember when . . . "

ENTRY THREE, 9/12/83:
THE NEW KID

Melvin Porter, the kid who always tries to kiss me, is the only new kid we got this year. He is real tall and he runs into walls and falls over his own feet a lot. He wears tennis shoes without shoestrings. The waist in his pants comes almost up to his armpits, how, I don't know, but that's OK because his tee-shirts are too short anyway. His glasses fall down his nose so he is all the time pushing them back up.

I know he is smart because he gave me an answer once in math when I couldn't get it on my own and I am no dummy. He likes to read books during recess. He can juggle, too. The guys tease him because he won't play football with them.

Roger leaves Melvin alone now, at least when I'm around. He doesn't know I've renounced kicking and I'm not telling him. My mother always says, "What you don't know won't hurt you," and that holds true in this case. (In case you don't have a dictionary right by you, "renounced" means "sworn off.") At least no one picks on Melvin now, but him trying to kiss me all the time makes it hard for me to be nice. I don't want to be mean but I don't want to be kissed either.

Sometimes people can be really mean, me too. Sometimes we will get together and write nasty notes about other kids and pass those notes around. Sometimes we won't let someone use our combs and say no, we don't want their cooties. Sometimes we make up stories about who kissed whom. Sometimes we pick on new kids. I wonder why we are like that?

I know I like to have people be nice to me. I remember one time when Valerie, this rich girl with a chipped tooth who is in my room, said to me, "Your mom is so pretty, I don't see how you could end up so ugly."

If I hadn't been busy on the toilet, I would have hit her for sure, but she ran out before I finished. What she said really hurt my feelings and I felt ugly for a long time. I wonder why she had to say that? Now that I think about it, I could have asked Valerie why, since her parents are rich enough for her to have 100 dolls, does she still have a tooth that needs fixed. I really would like to know the answer to that question.

When I asked Ms. Montgomery about that she said people sometimes are nasty at school because of what happened at home and vice versa. Maybe that's why Valerie is so awful. Maybe her parents don't pay attention to her.

I wonder if adults are mean to each other, too. Maybe that's just the way things are in life. I hope not. It's kinda sad to think we'll never get any nicer to each other.

Even though we argue sometimes, Eddo and I have made a pact to be nice to each other. I can't imagine him being mean, ever. If he was, I don't know what I'd do. Whenever I feel sad, thinking about life or about not having a dad, Eddo knows and he tells me a joke to cheer me up, like the other night.

"Why didn't the skeleton cross the road?" he asked me.

"Oh, geez, not another joke, Eddo. I just ate dinner and I don't want to throw up."

"Come on, Sally Jo. Why didn't the skeleton cross the road?"

"All right. Why?"

"Because he didn't have the guts!"

I stuck my finger in my mouth and pretended to throw up, but Eddo knew I liked it.

Sally Jo's assignment for her future kids:

Why do you think we are mean to each other when we want people to be nice to us? What mean things have you heard people say?

ENTRY FOUR, 9/14/83:
MORE ABOUT EDDO

Eddo's mother swears the gypsies came and stole her real son away because no son of *hers* could act the way he does. It's not unusual to be outside and hear her call, "Ed-MUND!" at least once an hour. When your parents use your real name, you know you're in trouble.

Eddo does keep busy. He never runs out of things to do. He likes to trick his dog, Duke, who is a mix of black lab and other happy stuff. He makes Duke jump for a piece of meat and at the last minute he switches spinach for meat and Duke gobbles down the spinach. You ought to see the "What was THAT?" look on Duke's face when he realizes he ate spinach. I think he has a look on his face anyway. Some people don't think animals can think, but I do. I think animals have feelings just like we do.

Eddo takes Duke everywhere, whether he's supposed to or not. He just tells Duke to sit and Duke sits, most of the time, in front of the optometrist's office, the cleaners, the grocery store, or the baseball field.

Duke forgot to sit one time when we went to the river. He plunged in up to his neck and it's a good thing it was a hot day. Eddo ran him a lot to dry him off before bringing him back home. His mom does not like a wet, muddy dog in the house.

Eddo didn't want a lecture from his father which always happens if Eddo does something wrong.

"Edmund, your father will hear about this," his mother says.

Actually, though, it's Eddo who hears about it. He'll do anything to avoid one of his father's lectures. I know I would. His father always explains everything so calmly and coolly, and tells Eddo how much he loves him and what a neat person he thinks Eddo is and how disappointed he is by Eddo's latest slip-up until Eddo is crying so hard he can't even talk. Parents don't need to hit their kids to get them to behave. Just talk logically for an interminable amount of time. (If you don't have a dictionary by you, "interminable amount of time" means so long you can see rocks move.)

Eddo and I are blood brothers even though I'm a girl. Eddo knows plenty about me and if he revealed any of it to my mom, all my hopes of becoming an adult someday would disappear. If she knew I moon Melvin Porter, the new kid at school, when he keeps riding by me on his dorky bike even after I told him to get lost, I'd be a goner.

Eddo and I have been through so much together. We know the worst about each other, but we're still friends. I can't imagine getting through life without Eddo and his Sherlock Holmes adventures and the trouble that Duke gets him into.

For example, Eddo keeps trying to teach Duke to roll over and play dead. Eddo rolls over with his legs and arms straight up in the air, his eyes crossed and his mouth wide open and his tongue hanging out. Duke just sits there with his tongue hanging out, drooling. At least he gets the tongue part of it right.

Eddo's mom yells at him for all the grass stains on the back of his jacket and jeans but he doesn't give up trying to teach Duke. I always wonder who will be the most persistent in the end, Duke or Eddo.

Dogs are supposed to be a person's best friend, but I'd take Eddo over my dog Trixie any day, even if he can't pull me on my roller skates the way Trixie does. I can't imagine what it would be like if he wasn't my friend.

Without Eddo, I would miss all the laughing we do together. We always get into trouble when we are together. Not bad trouble but adults yelling at you trouble. I wonder what trouble we will get into this year?

Sally Jo's assignment for her future kids:
  Who is your best friend and what do you know about each other?

ENTRY FIVE, 9/21/83:
ROMANCE

Eddo told me yesterday that his mom and dad tease him about my being his girlfriend and his dad makes kissing noises until he pleads with them to stop. We are annoyed with how they don't understand us. Just because we're together all the time doesn't mean we're romantic like in those books Eddo's mom is always sighing over.

I have sworn off boys and love for a long time, maybe until I am in high school. I have more to do than stand around holding hands with some guy. Maybe that's because I had lousy luck the one time I was in love.

In the third grade, before I knew Eddo, I really liked the boy who lived across the field from me. Jerry Holliman was shorter than me, but really, really cute, and he had a big German Shepherd. Even though I would've thrown away my life for Jerry (I peeked at what they say in those romance books Eddo's mom reads.) he hated my guts. Eddo's mom calls that "unrequited love."

That means someone doesn't like you back. I was in love with Jerry's curly hair and the fact he always knew the answer to everything. I kept following him home from school, walking fast to catch up with him. He kept running to get away from me. Some days he started earlier for home than I did, some days later, but there I always was, right behind him.

One day he turned around and shouted, "Quit following me!"

"I can't help it," I said. "I have to go this way home, too. I have to go by your house before I can cross the field to my house."

"Just stay away from me," he said.

"I'm not following you on purpose," I said, but I was and we both knew it.

Finally, he got his mom to pick him up from school. I got the message but I didn't like it. I made myself ignore him from then on.

Right now I feel like that romantic stuff is a big waste of time. How do people get to be who they are, rich and famous, if they waste time kissing?

Lisa is always talking about kissing. She has blond hair and everyone points out how pretty she is. She knows it, too. She doesn't even have freckles. Every word out of her mouth is either boys, boys, boys, or kissing, kissing, kissing. It makes me sick.

Eddo has kissed a girl before, but I don't know the particulars. He started to tell me and I put my hand up and said, "Stop. I don't want to see the picture of you kissing a girl in my head all day."

I do know that my friend Cindy practices kissing in her hall mirror because one day I came in the front door when she was doing it.

"AIEEE!" she yelled. "Sally Jo, you scared me to death sneaking around like that."

"I just came in the front door," I said. "How is that sneaking around? If I came in your bedroom window, then that might be sneaking around but not the front door."

"Well, knock next time and don't you dare tell anyone what you saw."

"OK, no big deal, but what were you doing? Are you planning to kiss someone?"

"Maybe. Someday. I just like being prepared. In case."

I guess if I need to know anything about kissing, I can ask Eddo or Cindy. I try to ignore Lisa.

Melvin Porter keeps telling everybody he wants to kiss me. That makes me want to throw up. Why doesn't he want to kiss someone who wants to, like Lisa? Or somebody who practices kissing, like Cindy? Besides, I vow not to let a boy's lips touch mine until I'm 14 or 15 and absolutely have to.

Anyway, I refuse to worry about romance because my mom gave me a book to read and believe me, life gets really complicated with body parts and hormones and sex. I don't mind waiting. I'd rather all that stuff just didn't happen but Mom says there's no way out of it. I think I'm lucky to have a mom who talks to me about grown-up things like I'm almost adult. I'm not so lucky about Melvin Porter. I'd like to smash his face in, only I promised Ms. Montgomery I wouldn't hit anymore. It sure is hard being mature.

Sally Jo's assignment for her future kids:

Write about how you used to love someone the way I loved Jerry Holliman.

Write about a situation where you chose to be mature and what was hard about that decision.

ENTRY SIX, 10/01/83: THE SCHOOL DANCE

I'm going to murder Melvin Porter. He tried to kiss me again last Saturday night. I feel queasy every time I think about it. Besides which, the whole night was a disaster. It was our first sixth grade dance that Mrs. Warren, the PE teacher planned, along with Lisa's mother.

For weeks we've been learning dancing, the two-step, the four-step, and the polka, in PE. Melvin Porter dances the three-step no matter what. He has sweaty hands and garlic breath. He always asks me to dance. The boys have to say, "May I please have this dance?" and the girls have to say, "Thank you. I'd be delighted." How dorky! Nobody means a word of it. When Mrs. Warren isn't looking, the boys try to step on our feet. During one of our classes earlier this year I stumbled and fell all over Roger's feet. I said, "Excuse me," and changed partners fast.

We do our dancing in the gym which stinks like old sweat and leftover farts. The music echoes due to the high ceiling so I'm never sure if I'm really moving on the beat or the echo of the beat. I am not alone in this torture.

Dancing is not much fun for Eddo either. Every time he takes a step, the top of his head hits the bottom of Shirley's chin. Bop, bop, bop. Once when we were doing a polka, Eddo's head hit Shirley's chin so hard it made her mouth fly shut and she bit her tongue. She yelled at Eddo, who yelled back at her that he didn't much like the sore spot on the top of his head her chin was making, and she was probably giving him brain damage.

After all that yelling, she keeps asking him to dance and he keeps saying yes, so I guess it's their problem to work out. If they aren't going to follow the "who asks whom" rule, I'm not getting involved.

I'll bet no sixth-graders anywhere in the world other than here have to go through this agony. The only good part is that the boys have to stay six inches away from the girls. I wish Melvin Porter would stay six *countries* away from me.

Our music teacher, Mrs. Dominick, plays the piano on practice days, so we don't even have any good music to dance to, just her old-fashioned stuff from the dark ages when she was a kid. Probably back when she danced, her big behind bumped into people and boinged them across the room. Boing! Boing! Boing!

Mrs. Dominick is nearly bald, her pink scalp shining through in patches covered by a few strands of hair dyed jet black. She must do it herself because there are stripes of white hair showing so she ends up looking like a diseased skunk.

As I said, the big dance in the cafetorium was last Saturday afternoon. The cafetorium smells better than the gym, more like last week's spaghetti, and the janitor doesn't have to worry that our shoes will get crud all over his shiny gym floor. There's linoleum on the cafetorium floor and it's used to a lot of kid slop.

All the PTA mothers got together and decorated with pink crepe paper streamers and white paper bells left over from someone's wedding. They folded up the tables and pushed them over to one side of the room. They pushed one of the tables over in front of the middle of the stage and covered it with a pink paper tablecloth. The teachers sat in front of the table so they could look over the floor.

We had to attend this dance in order to receive our PE grade. Mrs. Warren would be watching us and grading, a sure thing to take all the fun (if there was going to be any) out of it. At least there would be refreshments so we had something to look forward to. Parents were encouraged to attend but my mom said she had papers to correct.

"You can walk there since it's so close and I know you will behave appropriately," she said. She trusted me a lot more than I do.

No one was supposed to go with dates.

"Let's keep our children young as long as possible," Mr. Ellis, the principal, said to the PTA mothers, of which my mom is one. She reported back to me. "Besides, some of the children might be left out if they paired up, and that would not be good."

No one would go with Melvin, that is for sure, but I think that *would* be good.

Lisa's mom thought a date would be cute though, so she called Roger's mom and they fixed up a date. I could tell Lisa loved every minute of her datedom. She batted her eyelashes and flounced around like she thought she was a fairy princess. She even had pink painted fingernails.

Lisa's mom took pictures of Lisa's dress, and Roger's mom made him take Lisa a corsage and both moms took pictures. Lisa pretended to kiss Roger's cheek. I'll bet Roger kicked Lisa a good one later for that. He didn't look very happy at the dance. In fact, he looked dazed, like in movies when people look up and see an alien space ship hovering just over their heads and the light comes down and hypnotizes them.

I had my own troubles. I wanted to wear my jeans, but my mom said for once I could look more like a girl, and so I wore my dumb old wedding-funeral-church-important occasion-dress to make her happy. My belief is that if you are a girl you will look like a girl no matter what you are wearing. Clothes do not make you a boy or a girl, do they?

When Mom wasn't looking, I took my roller skates and I put them on outside of the cafetorium door before I went in, so I could move around the dance floor easier, and no boys could step on my toes unless they jumped up really high and that would catch a teacher's attention so they weren't going to do that. Mrs. Dominick tried to get me to take them off, but I said that my mom said I could wear them and she could call her to check it out if she wanted. I was pretty sure one teacher would not want to start a fight with another teacher and it worked. She quit bugging me. Still, she wrinkled up her lips and stared at me all night. She looked like a constipated fish.

Eddo brought Duke. Trixie was out visiting Uncle Jim at his farm, or I would've brought her to keep Duke company. He probably felt lonely being the only dog there. Dogs aren't allowed in the building, so Eddo made Duke sit outside by the bike rack. Shirley kept asking Eddo to dance and every time his head hit her chin, his glasses fell down farther on his nose.

Instead of keeping six inches away, Shirley got excited to be dancing with her one true love and threw her arms around Eddo's shoulders which put his face right in her chest so he couldn't breathe or see what was going on and his glasses got all twisted. Eddo said he wanted to sit down because he felt like he was going to faint from lack of air. I don't know what kept him from having a concussion.

Mrs. Dominick went over to Mr. Ellis and asked him to dance and he didn't look very happy about it. She danced by me, yakking, and leading Mr. Ellis, who nodded, his eyeballs darting to the walls and ceiling. His forehead was covered with sweat. They followed the "stay away from each other six inches" rule, except for them it was about two feet. Maybe he was afraid to step on her toes or maybe she thought he had bad breath.

Most of the boys stayed over by one wall, talking about cars and making fart noises in their armpits. The girls stayed over by the other wall, asking each other how they looked and who they thought the cutest guy was. I just listened because I knew this was good material for our class newspaper: "Cutest Guys at Saturday's Dance." I thought about rating the fart noises, too, but I don't think Mr. Wilson would let us put that in the paper.

The parents who came sat at the far end of the cafetorium in a couple of rows of folding chairs. Some of the ladies talked with each other and the men crossed their legs and folded their arms over their chests like they were just daring anyone to talk to them. They did not smile and kept looking at the clock. I'll bet they wanted to go make fart noises too but they had to act grown up instead.

Lisa's mom, Mrs. Warren with her clipboard and grade sheet, and Mrs. Dominick walked around and told kids to dance and so some of them did because they wanted to pass to the seventh grade. You do not want to get on a teacher's bad side, especially Mrs. Dominick's *back*side. Ha-ha-ha! Roger's mom and Mr. Ellis sat with their backs to the table that held the punch and cake, so they didn't see what I saw.

Duke got tired of waiting outside for Eddo, and he heard all the kids inside, so he came in to investigate. He must have been thirsty, because after he sniffed out all the corners behind the refreshment table, he smelled the punch, put his paws up on the table, and started lapping it up. I nonchalantly skated over beside him so no one would notice, and when I was close enough, I grabbed his collar and took him back outside. He was so happy to see me that his tail started wagging and I know he thought I was going to play.

"Bad Boy!" I told him. "Stay!"

His face got sad, and I swear a doggie tear rolled down his nose, so I gave him a big hug and some dog nose slime got on my dress, but that's OK. Maybe the snot won't wash out and I won't have to wear that crummy dress again.

I forgot all about the dog nose slime when I went back in to the dance and saw Roger's mom and Mrs. Dominick pouring themselves big cups of punch and saying how tasty it was. I laughed so hard I could barely get the story out to Eddo, and he went to tell all the other guys. They began laughing, and Lisa's mom and Mrs. Warren thought their dance was a success because everyone looked so glad to be there. Grownups should know that when a bunch of boys is laughing, it's probably not for the reason they think.

It was right after that, while I was standing by the doorway over by the parents, when Melvin Porter put his arms around me and kissed me, slobber and all, right on the lips!

"You look pretty," he said.

"Yuck!" I screamed. "What in the heck do you think you're doing? I don't want your gross cooties!"

I spat and wiped off my mouth and then pushed him away. I forgot I was on skates, though. He didn't move, but I did. I shot out backwards across the gym floor and bumped right into Mr. Ellis, who was bent over talking to Lisa's mom, so he didn't see me coming. I hit him hard and he dropped his cake and then fell on top of her. The next thing I knew, the cake was squished on her chest, Mr. Ellis's head was in her lap, and I was on the floor. My head swam and Lisa's mom screamed.

Lisa stopped flouncing and said, "Sally Jo, you have ruined my special date!"

All the kids laughed until Mrs. Warren looked at them with her evil eye. "Get back to business, all of you!" she said.

Mr. Ellis said, "Sally Jo Benedict, go to the office!"

I was plenty ticked at Melvin Porter, I can tell you, since he started it all. I think that *he* should have been sent to the office. When I opened my mouth to say so to Mr. Ellis, he said, "Do not say a word. Get to my office on the double and take off those roller skates immediately!"

He was trying to clean off Lisa's mother who was trying to get Lisa to stop blubbering. He wiped at Lisa's mom's chest with a couple of the paper napkins which were now greasy shreds. The more he yelled at me the harder he wiped. Lisa's mother turned away from Lisa's wailing and suddenly looked down at Mr. Ellis' hand, aghast.

"Stop that this instant," she said to him.

"Oh, I'm sorry," he said, and jerked his hands back fast. His face reddened. He got up and walked really fast to the garbage can and threw the napkins away and adjusted his suit jacket and frosting-smeared tie before turning around again.

Just at that moment, Eddo sneaked up to the record player somebody's parents had donated for the evening so we wouldn't have to listen to Mrs. Dominick persecute the piano—or us either. Of course, we'd rather have cassettes and a tape player, but if parents donate something, we have to accept it. Eddo took off the record that was playing and chose "Billie Jean" on Shirley's Michael Jackson record that everybody liked. Everyone ran out on the floor waving their arms in the air and shouting with the music, the way we *really* dance when Mrs. Warren isn't around.

Everyone was crazy glad to finally have a good time. Everyone except Mrs. Warren. She ran over to the record player to snatch the record off the turntable.

"Screeeeech," went the needle across the grooves. Everyone put their hands up to their ears. I'll bet Shirley was mad her record would now be ruined.

"Children, what do you think you're doing? This music is not acceptable!" she hollered. Everyone got quiet, even Mr. Ellis. "You are acting like little savages! That is quite enough!"

She could have called pigs with that yell. She called *us* savages?

I'm sure Mr. Ellis thought of how he'd rather be watching football on TV right now.

Little by little, Roger, who wanted to liven up the party now that Lisa wasn't hanging all over him, had sneaked over to a cluster of balloons decorating the wall. Just then he stuck the pin from his boutonniere into the whole cluster, one after another, bam, bam, bam! The noise frightened Duke who had sneaked back in for more refreshments and he jumped right onto the table, smack dab in the middle of the cake. All four of his legs sprawled out and every time he tried to stand up, his paws slid in the frosting and he fell into the cake again. When his mouth and nose noticed the cake he took a big, glomping mouthful and licked his doggie lips before trying to stand up again. A couple more attempts and he was so covered in frosting he looked like the Abominable Dogman.

Most of the moms just stared at the scene with their mouths open. Some of the dads sat there like before with their arms and legs crossed, except their eyes were closed like if they didn't see it, it wasn't happening. One dad who kept his eyes open laughed so hard he fell out of his seat like an out-of-control Gumby.

Lisa's mom started screaming again at a decibel that hurt Duke's ears so he barked and Lisa cried and Mrs. Dominick stuck her behind out and clapped her hands, shrieking, "Class, class!" and the boys held their sides and laughed so hard they must've peed in their pants.

All except Eddo, who realized he had to get Duke off the table, clean up the incriminating evidence and sneak away before Mr. Ellis got his wits about him. Even though the adults seemed to be reacting in slow motion, I didn't think Eddo and Duke were going to disappear in time to escape the long arm of the law.

I still had one skate to get off, but I hightailed it for the bench outside the office. I knew a lot of yelling was about to commence and I did not want to be a recipient of any of it.

Because of Duke, Eddo was sent to join me on the office bench. Duke ran outside, frosting flying off him. The rest of the kids got sent home.

Why is it the people who start trouble and bring everyone else into it never are the ones who get punished? Roger should have been sitting right beside us on that office bench but he got off scot-free from bursting those balloons and starting all the hullaballoo. Well, the second part of it, anyway. Everyone saw Melvin kiss me right in front of the parents but he never got in trouble either.

Eddo and I wondered if we would live another moment. We had to sit there until our parents came to get us and hear the whole story from Mr. Ellis. Eddo knew he was in for a night of lecture.

"Do you have any earplugs?" he whispered as we followed our parents out the door.

Mom was not happy about having to be called to the school, her being a teacher and all, but she did let me tell my side of the story. She is always fair that way.

When I told her what happened, she laughed.

"Sally Jo, you get in the strangest predicaments," she said. "However, you cannot tell anyone I laughed about this and you are grounded for a week for sneaking your skates to school. Get ready for bed."

Then she laughed some more.

After she finished laughing and was tucking me in, I asked, "Mom, why did Melvin Porter have to kiss me anyway?"

"Maybe he likes you, Honey, and he wanted you to know it."

She laid Rosco Teddy next to my head on the pillow.

"Ugh! Gross!"

"Well, you are pretty lovable—at least I think so."

"Yeah, but you're a mom. You're supposed to love me."

"Maybe Melvin can't help himself, Sally Jo. Liking someone is hard to explain. Sometimes we like people and we don't even realize it. Sometimes we like people and we don't even know why."

"I think that sounds stupid, Mom, and I'm not going to fall in love with anyone, ever," I said.

Mom just chuckled. "Poor baby," she said. "You won't be able to keep *from* it."

Some comfort she was. I wished I had Trixie to talk to. I would take dog nose slime over Melvin slobber any day.

———————————

Sally Jo's assignment for her future kids:

Has anyone ever liked you that you didn't like? What did you do about it? Why do you think they liked you?

ENTRY SEVEN, 10/03/83:
I USED TO THINK

Today, I walked to Eddo's to pick him up on the way to school. He was already out on the sidewalk, walking on his hands and jerking his feet around.

"What are you doing that for?" I asked him. He is graceful and I've told him before he should be a gymnast. But he says he doesn't want to wear tights, so I guess that's that.

"I'm tap-dancing on the sky," he said. "It's neat. Why don't you try it?"

So I did, and we went for about half a block that way until our hands got tired and sore from BB-sized pebbles sticking to them. My braids hung down too, and looked like little arms shooting out from my ears. You can see insects real good when your face is right down by them. You don't notice them at all when you walk right side up except if you are really concentrating, but then you run into other people and poles and stuff.

Do you ever wonder about ants' brains? People say their brains are so tiny, they can't think but I'm not sure I agree. They seem smart to me because I've watched them solve problems, like when I put a bunch of debris in the path where a lot of them are marching and they figure out how to go around. I know their brains are tiny but what if their brains are like computer chips with tons of memory so really they are just as smart as we are?

I saw an ant march through the grass like a bear through trees and I wonder if the ant thought he found a huge highway when he stumbled up onto the sidewalk. I bet when he saw my braid coming it was like when you sit inside your car in the carwash and those big brushes start flapping against your windshield. I flapped my head around like a carwash brush until I got dizzy and then I stood up on my feet and took a deep, deep breath and blew it right back out.

"Eddo, how do you suppose people breathe and swallow upside-down?"

"I don't know. Do I look like Mr. Science?"

"Let's see if we can eat upside-down too, OK? You first."

I trick him by saying "you first" all the time because he forgets that I was supposed to do the same thing, too.

Eddo will do anything to eat, so I got his peanut butter and salami sandwich out of his back pack and he took a bite. Yep, he swallowed just fine although he said he had to do it faster and harder than usual, and we decided to ask Mr. Wilson how that worked. Eddo wondered if you could pee upside-down too, but I said if he tried that in front of Mr. Mead's house, I would never speak to him again.

Mr. Mead is extremely particular about his lawn and flower garden, a real grouch where kids are concerned. He's not so nice to adults, either, now that I think about it. He cares about his flowers so much that at night he shines colored lights on them to show them off. At Mr. Mead's house it's Christmas outside all year long. Mom says that all he needs is a pink flamingo and she threatens to stick one in his lawn when he's not home. She says the only problem is he'd probably like it and then there'd be no fun for her.

Mr. Mead yelled at Mom because she had a 4-foot wire fence installed around our vegetable garden. He said it was the wrong height but I think he just plain hated that fence. He called the city planner to complain, but when the city planner got to our house, she was a woman, and she loved Mom's fence and asked who built it because she wanted one just like it for her vegetable garden. Boy, was Mr. Mead mad. He said cuss words.

I say hello to him if he's out in his yard but that's all. Mom told me that she did not want to have him yelling at her about something *I* did.

Here is the weird thing about Mr. Mead. One day I saw him outside lying on his lounge chair. OK, I was spying through our hedge but only because I heard tinkling. I looked through the laurel bush to see him holding a teeny brass bell. He tinkled it once and out came Mrs. Mead, her brown hair teased up and sprayed, wearing a cotton sundress, bringing him a drink. He took a sip and then he tinkled the bell two times and out came Mrs. Mead bringing him his slippers. I couldn't believe she was smiling both times. Tinkling went on that whole afternoon. When I told Mom about it later that night, she rolled her eyes so hard they almost got stuck on her forehead.

I usually never see Mrs. Mead outside. She's probably inside lying down because she's so tired from all that tinkling. Or maybe he keeps her tied up in the corner until he needs something. All's I know is, he isn't nice to kids or women.

"Hey, Sally Jo," Eddo said, and I stopped thinking about Mr. Mead. Eddo's face was all red from being upside down.

"What?"

"What did they call the thief who fell in the vat of liquid gold that he was trying to steal?"

"Uhm . . . the liquidator?"

"No."

"I don't know then." I never guess the right answer so I usually always say that I don't know right away so I can hear the punchline faster. "What did they call him?"

"Gilty. Get it? Like guilty, only covered with gold, like he was gilded."

"That's a pretty good one, Eddo."

"I made it up myself."

"I can tell. But you know what, Eddo? I read a story once where a lady got covered with gold paint for a circus freak show and her pores couldn't breathe and she died."

"Oh, cripes, Sally Jo. Quit being so technical. It's just a joke."

When we got to the playground, Shirley grabbed Eddo's arm and took him off in a corner, so I went to talk with Cindy. I could see Roger and Lisa and their friends talking and staring at me.

"Hey, Sally Jo. What happened Saturday after the dance? Did you get the paddle?" Cindy asked.

Oh, here we go, I thought. I hoped I wouldn't have to answer these questions all day long.

"Listen, I can't bear to talk about it. I've never been so mortified in my life, standing in front of everyone with Melvin Porter's slobber all over my face. Eddo and I got a big lecture from Mr. Ellis, and I had to apologize to Lisa's mom although I don't know what for since Mr. Ellis was the one who fell over on her."

"Was your mom mad?"

"My mom was good about it, but Eddo's dad lectured him for two hours after they got home. I don't want to talk about it anymore. My lips are sealed."

"Unless Melvin kisses you again," Cindy said.

I glared at her. "NOT funny." If I don't tease her about her freckles, she shouldn't bug me about Melvin. Neither one of us can help what happens to us.

Suddenly, I felt a tug on my sleeve, and when I turned around, it was HIM—Melvin Porter. We were face to face. Cindy stared with her mouth hanging wide open.

"Can you believe him?" Cindy said.

"What do you WANT?" I shouted at him. "Stop touching me! Back away! Haven't you caused enough trouble already?"

"I-I-I just wanted to say I'm sorry and I hope that you're not mad at me," He stammered.

"I'm plenty mad at you, Melvin. That was a rotten thing to do and you got me in a lot of trouble. I want you to just leave me alone. You stay out of my way from now on."

I thought about my promise to Ms. Montgomery but I clenched my fist in spite of myself. It was all I could do to remain mature. Melvin said nothing. He just stood there watching his foot scrape back and forth in the dirt.

"DO YOU UNDERSTAND ME, MELVIN?" I screamed.

I know my face was red because it gets that way when I yell and when I'm embarrassed which I started to be again because I saw everyone on the playground noticing us.

Melvin kept staring at the ground and his face was red, too. "Yeah, OK," he said and he looked around like he didn't know what to do next.

Just then I saw Eddo and stormed off toward him, leaving everyone standing there whispering and staring at Melvin.

"What was that all about?"

"Never mind, just come on," I said, and we went to our room to ask our teacher, Mr. Wilson, about swallowing upside down. He explained how the throat muscles keep on working even against the force of gravity.

"Can people pee upside down?" Eddo asked.

"I believe it's highly probable. However, if you are going to experiment to find out, please don't do it at school," Mr. Wilson said, smiling. "You may report your findings to me at a later date."

The bell rang and after we took lunch count and had announcements, Mr. Wilson said that it was time to work on our class newspaper. This is my favorite part of class because I like to write. I guess you can tell that.

Eddo and I have our own column and the topic we choose changes every issue. I think I'll be a reporter when I grow up. I like to ask people questions and if you do it because you're writing a story, they don't tell you to mind your own business.

In our September column, Eddo and I wrote about different kinds of dogs because we wanted to find out what kinds Trixie and Duke are. Our librarian, Mrs. Orton, helped us to find some books about breeds of dogs and we found out that Duke is a Black Labrador and Trixie is a combination of something, probably German Shepherd and Collie.

This month we decided to write about what people used to think when they were little kids. We were so dumb it is funny. Here's our newspaper column of what people used to think:

I USED TO THINK

by
Sally Jo Benedict and Eddo Richards

Hilda Benedict, my grandma, who was born before pantyhose: I used to think that there were little people singing in the radio and I wondered how they made the song sound the same every time. This was when I was five, before TV was made.

Shirley: As I am Catholic and go to church every Sunday, I have known the Our Father (a prayer) since I was very small. One part says, " . . . and lead us not into temptation." I used to think it said, " . . . and lead a <u>snot</u> into temptation."

Mr. Wilson: When I was young, I used to think I could fly. I climbed up on my jungle gym and jumped off all the time. I put leaves in my hands, wore a cape, and flapped my arms. My mom told me that I couldn't fly and that I should quit, but I wouldn't give up. I never did fly. I guess my mom was right.

Lisa: I used to think that there were monsters and snakes living under my bed. When I went to bed, I'd crawl under the covers. I wouldn't even get up if I had to go to the bathroom because I knew if I set one foot on the floor, something would grab it.

Mr. Richards (Eddo's dad): I used to think that the center of wood was filled with sawdust and when a saw sliced open a board, the "filling" spilled out. It never occurred to me that sawdust was actually ground wood from the powerful saw blade.

Cindy: I used to think that if you turned off the TV in the middle of a show, you could turn it back on the next day and finish watching it. Then my mom told me the show continues playing whether you watch it or not. You have to tape it if you want to watch it later.

Mrs. Warren: I used to think if you looked down the holes where flowers go at the cemetery, that you could see the dead person down that hole.

Jim Benedict (my uncle): I used to think that when we went for a drive in the car the roads turned the way we wanted to go, instead of us turning the way the roads went.

Neal: I used to think that pine trees swayed in the wind because that's how they got water up to the limbs. That's what my big brother told me and I didn't know any different until my mom got mad at him for saying that.

You know, all these "I used to think's" got me to thinking. If we all believed these things when we were kids, are there things we think now that aren't right, too? Are we going to find out when we're old, like 16 or 18, that we thought something stupid when we were 11 or 12?

I wonder if people go through life being stupid and then finding out. I don't think Mom is stupid but she does do strange things every once in awhile. For instance, she will always eat the middle out of things like cornbread or lasagna and leave the ends for me. And she has told me that grown-ups make mistakes just like kids. She subtracted wrong in her checkbook and had to go take some more money to the bank once.

Maybe that's what my mom means when she tells her students that we're all kids—some of us are just older. But I wonder. Is there an age when we're perfect, when everything we think is really true?

Oh. One other thing. There was another "I used to think" I didn't tell you about. We didn't put it in our column. It said, "I used to think Sally Jo Benedict was nice because she stuck up for me once. Then I did something dumb and now she doesn't like me at all." That was written by Melvin Porter.

Sally Jo's assignment for her future kids:
Write about something you used to think when you were younger.

ENTRY EIGHT, 10/12/83:
MR. WILSON

Eddo's and my teacher this year is Mr. Wilson. I like him a lot. So does my mother, I'm beginning to think. She visits him sometimes in his classroom after school and it's not because there is a teacher meeting or because I'm in trouble either, although I thought that at first.

I ran home and hid in my bedroom the first time I saw her in Mr. Wilson's classroom after school, and I didn't come when she called me for dinner. I starved myself for nothing though. When I finally did come to eat, I could barely swallow because I thought I was going to get yelled at after dinner.

Mom read that it's bad to yell at kids during dinner because it upsets them and they get stomach aches, so she waits until after dinner. Except when I do something wrong, I keep thinking about what's waiting for me after dinner, and I get a stomach ache anyway.

"Are you going to yell at me?" I finally asked, because the suspense was killing me and I couldn't enjoy my corn dogs. (I know, corn dogs are not good for you but Mom allows me to eat them once a month as a treat.)

"Why would I yell at you, Sally Jo?"

"Oh, nothing."

"Did you do something I don't know about?"

"I don't think so," I said. "I saw you in Mr. Wilson's classroom this afternoon when I stayed late with Eddo to work on our video so I guessed I must be in trouble."

"Oh," Mom said, and she blushed. "No, that's not it."

"What were you doing there if I'm not in trouble?"

"Never mind, Sally Jo. It didn't concern you. Just eat your corn dogs."

She always tells me to eat my dinner when I bring up stuff she doesn't want to talk about. Usually, the subject of her boyfriends and romances. She knows I get upset because I think my mom should love only my dad even though he's dead. I know that's impossible but that's how I felt until I talked with Ms. Montgomery. Now, I'm trying to be more mature about that feeling.

"Are you going to have a date?"

"Sally Jo, I said I do not wish to talk about it. I'm going to go correct papers. Clean up your dishes when you've finished. Then do your homework."

Boy, I wish I didn't have to talk about stuff when I didn't want to. I can just hear myself saying, "Mom, I do not wish to talk about it. Now go correct your papers. And clean your room, too. It's a disgusting mess."

Wouldn't it be funny if things were turned around just for a day? I saw a movie like that once, but none of the characters had a good time. I guess we're just supposed to be who we are, no matter what.

I hope Mom does like Mr. Wilson though and that surprises me. I like the way he teaches history. We acted out the signing of the Declaration of Independence and I got to be Thomas Jefferson. I dressed up in jeans and a frilly white shirt and a red scarf tied around my neck for a tie. He took pictures of us and we got to keep them. I have mine on my dresser.

We are building a car out of cardboard, but I don't think it will have a real engine in it.

I like the way Mr. Wilson teaches geography. I have learned a lot about places like Mexico and New Zealand and Tasmania. We don't just memorize capital cities and exports.

He brings in his friends from those places who are going to school in the U.S. and they let us ask anything we want about where they live, like do they have McDonald's there and what is school like for kids our age.

Do you know the kids in Tasmania call erasers "rubbers"? And kids in England call sweaters "jumpers"? You have to be careful what you say in other countries or you can get in big trouble.

My favorite part of the day, though, is when we write. I like deciding what topics to write about in our class newspaper. We print it up ourselves once the school secretary types it for us. I already wrote about that, though.

I wonder if Mom and Mr. Wilson will go on a date. Oh, gosh, I wonder if they will kiss. Euwwww! Barf! At least my mom won't have to practice on a mirror like Cindy since she got plenty of kissing practice with my dad. That was awhile ago, though. I wonder if she remembers how.

Mr. Wilson doesn't look anything like the men on the front cover of Eddo's mom's romance novels. He doesn't have wavy locks flowing to his shoulders and he doesn't wear billowing white shirts open to reveal disgusting chest hair topped with a golden chain. He has short, brown hair fluffed over on one side and sometimes a piece of it falls down right in the middle of his forehead. He shaves, but he has a stubbly mustache—not one of those curlicue ones, but light and feathery. He wears suits and ties except for Fridays when he wears a polo shirt since it's the last day in the work week. That's when I can see the muscles in his arms so I think he must be strong.

When he's working on something with us and we're all thinking, he hums. Sometimes he just bursts out singing and we laugh. He has a good voice, not like Michael Jackson's but deeper, like Lionel Ritchie's.

All day long he eats breath mints and I'm so glad about that. Nothing I hate worse than stinky teacher breath when they lean over to help you.

I wonder how my mom would describe Mr. Wilson. I wonder if Mr. Wilson has been going to visit my mother sometimes in her classroom after school. I wonder if Mr. Wilson knows how to kiss. Now I am going to imagine him kissing a mirror every day in class. That is not a good picture to have in my head.

———————————

Sally Jo's assignment for her future kids:

Write about your favorite teacher. Use all the sense words—taste, touch, smell, sight and sound. Tell why you like that teacher. Then do the same thing for a teacher you do not like.

ENTRY NINE, 10/15/83:
THE CASE OF THE STOLEN WIENIES

I love spending October Saturdays lying on a chaise lounge in the back yard, looking up at the cloudless blue skies and letting the sun wash over my body in little waves of warm. I try to forget the snow is coming. Sometimes I read and sometimes I just close my eyes and daydream. Usually I smell Mr. Mead's barbecue because he cooks outside if the Saturday weather is nice. In October, the breeze blows and drifts of steak or chicken air go up my nose. Yum. Today it's wienies.

Trixie lies beside me and once in awhile licks my hand to let me know she's still there. If she sees a bird, she'll go chase it or do some of the other doggie things she likes to do, but she always comes back like a little kid checking in with her mom.

Speaking of moms, mine is usually in the house at her desk correcting papers which takes up most of her Saturdays. She comes out to enjoy the sun for a few minutes, but then she feels guilty and goes back inside. I am not going to be a teacher because I like the sun too much and correcting papers does not look like fun.

I mention all this, because something else has been going on with Eddo and me besides writing our column. Trixie has been at my uncle's for a week because of what happened last Saturday.

Last Saturday I was out in the back yard relaxing and getting warm, smelling Mr. Mead's barbecue next door, when I heard a bunch of yelling and tinkling going on over there. Mrs. Mead came out in her poufy hairdo, high heels and white apron and then I heard Mr. Mead yell, "I have had enough! I'm going to put a stop to this once and for all!"

I know it's not polite to eavesdrop, but I couldn't help it. I wondered what made Mr. Mead so mad. Just then our doorbell rang, and someone started pounding on our door. I ran in the house, and when I answered the door, there was Mr. Mead, standing there in his green and yellow plaid Bermuda shorts. His legs were all gray and black kinky hairy. I'm sorry I saw that up close.

"Sally Jo Benedict," he yelled, "your damn dog stole my wienies!"

"What are you talking about?" I said.

"I was barbecuing wienies. I had to go in the house for a second, and when I came back outside, all the wienies were gone. Your damn dog took them!"

"She did not," I said, lifting up my chin and squinting my eyes.

"Where is she?" Mr. Mead asked, sticking his stubbly snout inside our house.

"I don't know," I admitted.

"Well, I do. She stole my wienies and she's somewhere eating them."

"She did not." I put my hands on my hips and held my ground. "She was here just a second ago."

Even though I was angry with Mr. Mead for accusing Trixie

of stealing his food, and a little bit scared at his yelling, it was all I could do to keep from laughing. First of all, his red face was squinched up like faces get in werewolf movies when the guy is changing into a wolf. His hairy arm pumped up and down to emphasize every other word and I hoped he didn't get too excited and hit himself in the head with his hand.

But what struck me as really funny was a grown man, especially a grouch like Mr. Mead, shouting the word "wienies." This is because when Eddo was in the fourth grade he used to say this kind of naughty joke: "Guess what. I have four knees. (And then he'd point.) Left knee, right knee, hine-knee, and wee-knee!"

Right when I was thinking of his joke, Eddo arrived.

"What's going on?" he asked. I think if I'd seen Mr. Mead yelling at me, I would have hidden in the hedge until he went home, but Eddo is usually fearless.

"Aha!" Mr. Mead shouted when he saw Eddo. "Maybe it was *your* damn dog who was the culprit. Yes, that makes sense to me. That big black beast stole my wienies."

"He was barbecuing." I filled Eddo in on the situation.

"Duke's tied up at home," Eddo stated matter-of-factly.

"I'll just bet," Mr. Mead said as if he didn't believe a word of it. "That damn dog's always into mischief."

He would've gone on forever, but my mom came out of her study to see what all the noise was.

"Mr. Mead, good heavens! Please don't swear in front of these children. Get hold of yourself. If they say their dogs didn't steal your wienies, then they didn't. What about Yvette? Maybe she has your wienies."

Yvette is Mr. Mead's Pomeranian. Pomeranians are small dogs about 5-7 inches tall at the shoulder with long, silky hair, pointed ears, and a bushy tail turned over the back. Eddo and I learned that in our research for our newspaper column about dogs, the one I told you about, remember? Mr. Mead keeps Yvette's toenails painted red and puts little satin bows in her hair. When he lets her out in the morning, she comes over and poops in our yard, right by the Japanese Maple tree that is now dead.

"Yvette did not steal my wienies!" he shouted. "Unlike your dogs, Yvette is well-mannered and civilized. Besides, there is no way in hell she could reach the barbecue."

"Mr. Mead, I'm sorry you lost your wienies, but you're not going to get them back standing at my door and swearing. You are being rude to these children. Now go home and calm down."

"To hell with these children! And no woman is going to tell me what to do . . . "

Mr. Mead would've probably kept on yelling, but my mom said, "Good bye, Mr. Mead," firmly, and closed the door.

"Have a nice day!" Eddo said, and we all laughed.

Duke really was tied up and Trixie was in the back yard when I checked. I smelled her breath, but it just smelled like regular dog's breath and not wienies. I wonder if dogs burp after they eat wienies the way I do.

Eddo and I knew our dogs were not to blame and we decided to think of a way to prove it. After he had a couple of chocolate chip cookies, Eddo said he was going home to put on his thinking cap, and I know he meant that stupid Sherlock Holmes hat.

That night my mom and I had a talk about what to do.

"Jim is coming tomorrow," Mom said. "Maybe we should have him keep Trixie at the farm again until this whole thing blows over. Then Mr. Mead won't be over here yelling in case his barbecued food disappears again."

"Yeah, I don't like Trixie to get accused of stuff she doesn't do. It's bad enough to be a kid and have that happen to you. I know how she feels."

"Trixie is a good dog, Sally Jo. We'll just take care of the situation by having Jim take her for awhile. She loves to romp around out there, and Mr. Mead will have to direct his accusations elsewhere. And we won't have to be subjected to his disgusting swearing."

Swearing is pretty funny stuff actually. The words that people use to swear are stupid really. Think about it. Most swear words have to do with body parts or bodily functions. Wouldn't it be funny if people swore by saying, "Oh, Elbow!" or "Sneeze!" or "Spit!"?

In Mr. Wilson's class we learned that swear words in other countries are different from ours. Well, he didn't plan to tell us that, of course, but when his friends who live in other countries came to talk to us, we asked them about their swear words. That's just one of the things we're interested in. In France, to say the nastiest thing to another person, you call him a cow. If we did that here, it wouldn't mean anything at all. They also say, "Sacred blue!" for a cuss word. Can you imagine saying, "Holy yellow!" or "Blessed pink!"?

When I was two years old, I had my own swear words and I still remember them because my mom wrote them down in my baby book. They were "Shocken" and "Goshen." Don't ask me how I thought of those words, but Mom said I used them in all the right places.

Why do people have to swear anyway? Mom says it's because

they lack a good vocabulary and don't take the time to learn words that are more effective and meaningful. I think that's an English teacher answer. Besides, when she stubs her toe, she doesn't take the time to think of effective and meaningful words. You should hear what she says.

What I think about swearing is that it helps people to release steam when they're angry. Think about all the cuss words you know. That's what I did. I made a list and here's what I found out: They have sounds like "Sh," "Tuh," "Puh," and "Duh," in them, and all those sounds release air when you say them. I know because I said them into a mirror one day just to see, and it got all cloudy from my breath. My theory is that when an angry person releases all that air, he or she feels better. And that's why people swear. Maybe Eddo and I should research swearing for our next column.

If my theory is true, then Mr. Mead must have felt pretty good by the time he left our porch. Mom says he is not a good example of adult maturity for me to follow. I told her that I was old enough to figure that out.

The next day Eddo and I put our heads together and came up with a plan. The following Saturday Trixie would be at my uncle's and Duke would be at the veterinarian's getting his toenails clipped and his shots. If anything was stolen from Mr. Mead's barbecue, our dogs would be innocent. And we were going to get proof of who the thief was because we knew that Mr. Mead would never believe us otherwise.

That next Saturday Eddo came over and we waited in my back yard until we smelled Mr. Mead's barbecue. Then we crept over to the hedge and positioned ourselves so we had a clear view of his back yard. That was necessary for our secret weapon—Eddo's dad's Polaroid camera. The minute anyone or anything stole Mr. Mead's food, we'd snap a picture and a few seconds later, we'd have proof.

Mr. Mead came out and put two steaks on his barbecue. The smell drove me crazy because we'd been stuck in the hedge past lunchtime. "Maybe I'll go steal that steak myself!" I whispered to Eddo.

Mr. Mead sat down in his lawn chair with a stick across his lap, waiting for invaders. Yvette ran around and around him, jumping up and down and yipping, the way Pomeranians do. He kept saying, "Good doggie," "Sweet Baby," and stuff like that.

Once he tinkled his bell, and Mrs. Mead brought him out a glass of something in ice cubes.

"He's so lazy," Eddo whispered.

After awhile Mr. Mead's phone rang in the house and he tinkled his bell, once, twice, a third time, then a whole lot of tinkles, but still Mrs. Mead didn't answer the phone. He said some swear words to make himself feel better about having to get up, I guess, and went in to answer the phone himself.

That is when the thief went into action. She got up on the picnic table, first the seat and then the top, walked across it to where the barbecue was, and snatched one of the steaks. In a flash, she jumped down the same way she got up and ran for the hedge some distance from where we were.

"Did you get it? Did you get it?" I asked Eddo.

"You bet I did," he said. "Super sleuth goes into action. Just a second."

We waited for what seemed an eternity and then the picture began to emerge.

"Hooray! Yeah!" we said in unison until we noticed Mr. Mead standing above us brandishing his stick.

"What the hell do you two kids think you're doing?" he shouted. "So you're the ones stealing my food. Where's my steak?"

"We don't have your steak," Eddo said, backing up into the hedge for protection.

"Then your dogs do," Mr. Mead said, "because one of my steaks is gone. Just turn my back for a second and this is what happens. Damn worthless kids and their dogs, anyway!"

"For your information, our dogs aren't even around this afternoon. Trixie's on the farm, and Duke is at the vet's. But we do know where your steak is," I said.

"Oh, yeah? Where?"

"Take a look at this," Eddo said, giving him the picture.

Mrs. Mead came out of the house even though she hadn't been tinkled for and she looked at the proof, too.

"You owe these children an apology," she said.

"What? These fresh kids? Forget it," Mr. Mead said, throwing the picture down. "Besides, this doesn't prove their dogs didn't do it before."

"Yvette is over there in the corner of your yard," Eddo said, "eating your steak."

When Mr. Mead went to pick her up, she growled at him and bit his hand.

"Damn!" he shouted, and stormed past us into the house.

Mrs. Mead retrieved the photo from where it lay on the lawn and returned it to Eddo.

"I'm sorry," Mrs. Mead began to say, but Mr. Mead yelling from inside the house interrupted her.

"MIL-DRED! Get in here!"

Poor Mrs. Mead. I think I'll send her some earplugs.

When we told Mom what happened, she said, "That is a rude man and a good example of what not to be. He thinks what's important is what's on the outside so he keeps a spotless house and yard. Unfortunately, he pays no attention to what kind of person he is inside where it really matters."

"But, hey!" she continued. "You both had a good idea with the camera and he won't be so quick to blame other people now. You both will have to excuse me now. I'm going to take a bubble bath."

That's how my mom relaxes. She takes a bath and soaks sometimes for hours. Once she read a whole book while she was in the bathtub and she came out looking as wrinkled as a Shar Pei. Wish I would have had a Poloroid then!

Sally Jo's assignment for her future kids:

Write about a time when you were falsely accused of doing something. How did you prove you were innocent? How did you feel if no one believed you?

ENTRY TEN, 10/22/83:
A ROMANTIC DEVELOPMENT

Eddo and I got an A this week in Writing because of our "I Used to Think" newspaper column. We are going out to celebrate tonight with my uncle but that's not just because of getting an A. My uncle is staying in town with me because my mom and Mr. Wilson are having a date.

Here's how it happened: Mom came to school to get Eddo and me one day when we had to stay late to work on our column. See, after you ask people all the questions, which is called an interview, then you have to plan out how to write up their answers. Then you have to fit your writing into columns. The whole process is complicated and it takes some time, but if people like what you wrote, it's worth the time you spend.

When Eddo and I were cleaning up, Mr. Wilson and Mom talked. They started with the normal stuff like, "Hi, Tricia. Good to see you." And "Good to see you, too, Chet. How're you doing?"

Then when they thought we weren't listening, Mr. Wilson asked my mom to go out to dinner and a show. Eddo and I looked at each other and batted our eyelashes and stifled giggles.

Mom smiled all the way home. I wonder if she knew this

would happen when she came to pick us up? Maybe that's why Mr. Wilson told us we could work after school.

Eddo's mom came to visit tonight, right after we finished doing dishes.

She marched into the kitchen and looked point blank at Mom and said, "Well, Tricia?"

"Well, what?" Mom said.

"You know. How are things with Chet?"

"That's when Mom blushed and said, "Sally Jo, go clean your room."

"It's clean," I said.

"Then go get it dirty," she said.

"Huh?" I swear I don't understand parents at all. "But I want to hear about Chet, too," I said.

"Sally Jo!" Mom's voice got loud and she gave me her 'DO IT OR DIE!' look, which feels like her eyeballs are piercing mine. "You heard me. We wish to speak privately without little ears flapping around."

I almost reminded her that I didn't have little ears, that they were so big they had to be taped to my head when I was a baby because they stuck out so much which did not help one bit because they still do. But I kept quiet on that subject. I have learned not to be logical at times like this.

"Yes, Mom," I said, and I slogged up to my room and tried to listen to the conversation through the heating duct. Figuring out everything they said was hard to do, because they were giggling, but I did hear the name "Chet" which is Mr. Wilson's grown-ups-only name.

Sally Jo's assignment for her future kids:

Write about something your parents or friends say to you that doesn't make any sense.

ENTRY ELEVEN, 10/22/83:
PLAYING AROUND

Tonight Mom was going out on her date with Mr. Wilson so I was upstairs watching her put on eyeshadow and blush and mascara. I'm going to have to do that some day and I want to know how when the time comes which won't be until I'm 21 at least. I want to be prepared, though, so I paid attention to every detail. Why do women's mouths fly open when they put on mascara? Why do they put on lipstick and then put Kleenex between their lips and take some of it off?

Finally Mom told me to go away because I was making her nervous staring at her every move, and she was already nervous enough.

"Oh, Mom, I was just watching."

"That's what I mean Sally Jo."

As if I were going to divulge her beauty secrets and tell Mr. Wilson that she wears control-top pantyhose and fake fingernails. Not even wild rats could drag that out of me, even if I don't know any wild rats.

"I mean it, Honey. I want to be left alone for a few minutes. Go down and entertain your uncle. Isn't Eddo here yet?"

"OK. OK. But if you get a smudge someplace, don't blame me."

The minute he saw me, Uncle Jim sang, "Beautiful, beautiful brown eyes," which is a really old song. He makes me laugh and feel good. He likes being a kid around me. He likes to play around even though he's an adult and when he makes people laugh, he feels like laughing, too.

"Playing helps me to let off steam after a hard day, Brown Eyes," he told me once. "If adults would remember to play, they'd feel a whole lot better. Life's backwards. You should be able to be retired and play around with your kids. Then when they're grown, you could all go to work."

"Makes sense to me," I said, and it does. Otherwise, you end up missing each other.

He doesn't have kids because he works hard on his farm and he's not married. Sometimes I let him take Trixie home to keep him company. She likes to romp around on his farm.

My uncle pretends he's a dog sometimes, and he gets on his hands and knees and barks. Sometimes he'll be a cow and sing, "Oh, I'm just a cow and I want to live in a red barn, Moo, moo, moo." (Uncle Jim actually sounds like a cow singing), but mostly he chooses to be a dog.

Tonight Eddo, Uncle Jim, and I had to sit around and wait before we went to dinner at our favorite Chinese restaurant because my uncle wanted to meet Mr. Wilson. Then we were going to celebrate our A grade on our column.

"I just want to see what this Chet is made of—to see if he's OK for your mother to go out with," he said. He is protective of Mom because after all, he *is* her big brother.

"Oh, he's nice. Eddo and I like him a lot. He knows a lot of stuff."

"Well, he must be OK if you like him, but I still want to see for myself," my uncle said.

"Sally Jo, I don't want to go eat yet before I see how a teacher picks up someone to go out on a date," Eddo said.

I must admit I wanted to see that too, but I supposed it wouldn't be any different from anyone else since my mother is like a normal person most of the time. I mean, what is a teacher going to say, "I'm sorry, you can't go out with me unless you have your homework done"?

"I'm bored just sitting here," I complained to my uncle, and the next thing I knew, he was on all fours, barking and sniffing. I don't think Eddo had seen that before because he just stared for a minute and then looked at me. I shrugged my shoulders as if to say, "Who can tell why he's nuts?"

Eddo decided he liked the idea and all of a sudden he was barking too, and he pretended to lift his leg which made us all laugh. While they were barking, Trixie must've thought it was a dog convention because she came into the room and started licking their faces. By then she was barking. Eddo rolled over and played dead. My uncle started dancing on his knees with Trixie who looked like she wanted to get the heck out of there. Her tail was hitting Eddo in the face, so he crawled away and whined up at me. I put my hands over my ears and ran over to the front door, which was open, to get away from the barking chorus. I needed some fresh air. Mom came downstairs to see what the ruckus was about.

"Oh, Jim!" she said and put her hands up in the air like she was giving up. "What in the Sam Hill is going on here?" She looked at me and I shrugged my shoulders again. I'm used to

Uncle Jim barking. I also shrugged because who the heck is Sam Hill?

"Come on, join in," Uncle Jim said to us, and I was surprised to see Mom in her good clothes get on the floor and bark. Maybe she thought it would make her less nervous. Seeing Mom really got Eddo to laughing and he barked all the louder, like Mr. Mead's Pomeranian. His bark hurt my ears. Uncle Jim sounded like a St. Bernard, and Mom sounded like a Golden Retriever, or anyway what one looks like it would sound like. You can't tell much about barks from a resource book.

Everyone else acted like dogs, so I wanted to be different. I decided to be a cat and said meow and licked my arm. My sleeve was dry and hairy and I don't think I could lick my furry self all over like cats do for very long without my tongue going dry. How do they get enough spit?

I was going, "Meow, meow," and Trixie licked my face and looked like she didn't know who I was since I was speaking a foreign language. Then, just like in scary movies, a tingle went down my neck and I just knew someone was watching me. I looked over my shoulder, and Mr. Wilson stood there in the doorway, staring at everyone.

"Me-OH, GOSH," I said, and froze.

Then Eddo noticed him and stopped mid-yip. Then my mom noticed Eddo frozen like a statue and she turned her head around and saw Mr. Wilson. She stood up fast, brushing off her knees. Her face got white and then extremely red.

"Jim. Jim," she said, looking at Mr. Wilson while tapping my uncle on his shoulder, but he didn't hear her right away because he was still barking. Finally he noticed that he was the only one making any noise and he looked up.

We all stood there. I looked at Eddo and he looked at me. We looked at my mom and she looked at us. We all looked at my uncle and he looked at us and then at Mr. Wilson again. Trixie wagged her tail. Nobody made a sound.

Mr. Wilson suddenly burst out laughing. My uncle and Eddo and I joined in, and soon Mom did too until everybody was laughing and my mom rearranged her hair and dress.

"I did knock," Mr Wilson said.

Mom went over to him and took his arm, saying, "Hello, Chet. Come on in. Welcome to the doghouse. This is my brother, Jim. Jim, this is Chet, Sally Jo and Eddo's teacher."

"Pleased to meet you," my uncle said, getting up to shake Mr. Wilson's hand. "We were being a little crazy here."

"I wish I would have known," Mr. Wilson said. "I could've brought my dog bone biscuits. Hi, Sally Jo. Hi, Eddo. Or is it Fido and Fluffy?"

"Hello, Mr. Wilson," I said. "Jeez, I feel dumb," I whispered to Eddo.

"This is Trixie," I said to Mr. Wilson.

"Shake!" I said and Trixie gave Mr. Wilson her paw.

"Pleased to meet you, Trixie. You are the prettiest dog here. Well, except for Tricia."

What a sappy moment!

Then he said, "I seem to have shaken everyone's paw, so shall we wag our tails on out of here and head down to the pound, Tricia? I hear they have some great Gravy Train down there."

"You got yourself a deal." Turning to us she said, "You three have a good time tonight. If Fido and Fluffy give you any trouble, Jim, just put their muzzles on," and she and Mr. Wilson went out the front door, laughing.

"Gosh, I wonder what he thinks of us now?" I said. "He probably thinks we're nutso." I worried that he would stop going out with Mom if I wasn't perfect. I liked seeing her happy again.

"Better he finds out now than later," Uncle Jim said. "I don't think you have to worry. I think you're right. He's a nice guy. I'll bet it won't be too long before he's a regular down here at your doghouse, barking and meowing with the rest of us. How do you feel about that?"

Wow. I hadn't thought about anything past dating. I didn't mind Mom and Mr. Wilson going out but I didn't know about them staying in, here. How would that work, my teacher hanging out at my house?

"You know what?" Eddo asked, interrupting my thoughts. "Maybe your mom and Mr. Wilson are in puppy love. Get it?"

"Hey, that's a good one, Eddo. I always said you were a smart little mutt," Uncle Jim said, patting Eddo's head.

"Grrrr!" Eddo growled.

"Who's ready for dinner?" I said, changing the subject before barking started up again or before I had to think about how things between Mom and Mr. Wilson might develop.

"Me! Me!" Eddo shouted. "Me! Me!" Uncle Jim shouted, and off we went to Mei Yung's, leaving Trixie to guard the house.

Sally Jo's assignment for her future kids:

Describe some crazy things you do when you are playing around. What do your parents do when they are playing around (if they ever do)?

ENTRY TWELVE, 10/23/83:
CHOPSTICKS

At Mei Yung's Chinese Restaurant, the booths are covered in red vinyl upholstery and the plaster side walls are painted turquoise. The lights are orange, blue, or white plastic balls suspended from the ceiling. Nothing matches, not even the design on the dishes. Fake philodendrons are stuck in the room dividers. I know because I touched one to see if it was real and it felt rubbery. I can also tell the palm in the front window is phony because I can see the wires that attach the leaves to the stem. There are some soiled pictures of birds and butterflies on the wall. Either you get a smiling Chinese waitress who can't speak much English, or an American waitress dressed in a Chinese outfit. Uncle Jim says Chinese restaurants don't care much about good décor, just good food. In case you don't have a dictionary by you, "décor" is a word that means how a place is decorated, which is easy to remember, because "decorated" has "décor" in it. Get it?

Some décors have names, like "Early American" or "Victorian" or "Modern." The décor of Eddo's room could be called "Extreme Mess." His clothes are in a pile in the center of his room, except for the things that are hanging out of the drawers in his dresser. No wonder his socks never match. It scares me to look under his bed because sometimes green things are growing under there. He does experiments with food to look at under his microscope, but then he forgets and shoves the food under the bed with everything else. Of course, he never has to worry about snakes or witches under his bed, because there's no room. He did grow a weird crystal outer-space plant one time from of a lump of coal. Here's how:

* * *

Use a brick, pieces of coal, or cinders, and dampen them before placing in a shallow bowl. Rub the edge of the bowl with Vaseline to keep the plant from growing over the edge of the bowl. Mix thoroughly 6 tablespoons salt, 6 tablespoons liquid bluing, 6 tablespoons water, and 1 tablespoon household ammonia.

Pour this mixture over the brick, coal, or cinders. Add a few drops of Mercurochrome, or red or green ink. Place bowl in a dark place for a few days (like under Eddo's bed). A reaction will take place between the chemicals in the brick and the salt. The salt will assume a brilliant color.

After first growth has stopped, add a little more ammonia or wash thoroughly in warm water and start a new plant.

* * *

Be sure you tell your mom that you're growing this though, so she doesn't scream when she sees it, especially if it's under your bed. Better yet, ask her to help you make it because moms love to do this sort of thing once they get going.

Note to self: Wouldn't it be fun to do a column on what people had under their beds?

Now, regarding our Chinese dinner. I think Chinese food has the funniest names. Who can tell what it really means?

"Tim Shon Yuk Kow? What's that?" I asked, reading from the menu to Uncle Jim. "'Yuk' sounds like something you'd throw up."

"Moo Goo Gai Pan?" Eddo said. "'Moo Goo' sounds like cow pies," and that made us laugh about the other names.

"What's Moo Goo Foo Young?" I asked.

"That sounds like young cow pies as opposed to old ones," Eddo suggested.

"It's a mushroom egg pancake," my uncle told us. When he went to college he worked in a Chinese restaurant and learned what the names of the food really meant. He studied for school and then he came to work and studied some more.

"Is Au See Pie Kwat a dessert?" I wondered.

"No, it's really barbecued spare ribs."

"Here's one that sounds like lawyer food—Sieu Me."

"That's meatballs."

"I guess if you're depressed you can cheer up with some Chon Fun," Eddo said.

"Fried scallion cakes. See if you kids can figure out this one: Duck Yuk Cluck."

"Scrambled duck eggs?" Eddo guessed.

"Sweet and sour duck tongue?" That was my guess.

"Nope," Uncle Jim said. "I just made it up to see what you'd say. Ah, here's our waitress. Let's order. I'm starved."

"Ah so, ah so," Eddo said.

"Eddo, you dork! 'Ah so' is Japanese," I told him.

"Oh. Velly solly. Please excuse," Eddo said.

"Is no excuse for number one boy," the blonde waitress said, smiling. It's so embarrassing when they overhear what you're saying.

"That's for sure," Uncle Jim agreed, laughing.

Eddo frowned and studied the menu.

"Just remember," Uncle Jim told us, "that whatever you order, you have to eat with chopsticks. I'll show you how."

What's neat about some Chinese restaurants besides the name of the food is that you can order six different things and try them all out, and that's what we did. We had barbecued pork, sweet and sour spareribs, chicken chow mein, chop suey, Egg Foo Yung, and fried shrimp. And one big bowl of white rice.

"Sweet and sour is so strange," Eddo said. "I think you should have one or the other, either just sweet or just sour, but not both of them together."

"Pretty funny to hear that from somebody who eats peanut butter and salami sandwiches," I reminded him. "If you don't like your sweet and sour, that just means all the more for me."

After the waitress brought the food, we got to use spoons to put the stuff on our plates, but then we had to use our chop-sticks. Uncle Jim showed us how to hold them in our hands, but somehow they worked better for him than for us. The rice wouldn't stay on my chopsticks unless I got my mouth right down by my plate.

When Eddo got some chop suey in his chopsticks, he held it high in the air, turned his face up, and stuck out his tongue to reach it. The chop suey came out from between his chopsticks and splattered all over his cheek. Some of it, falling on his glasses, fogged them up.

I laughed so hard that somehow my chopsticks squeezed the piece of fried shrimp I had captured and it flew across our table and hit the lady at the table across from us in the head.

My eyes got big and I sucked in a lot of air, saying, "Oh!"

The lady turned to look at us and scowled, bugging out her eyes.

Uncle Jim, embarrassed, said, "Heh-heh. Excuse us, please. First time with chopsticks," and he gestured toward us.

"Sorry," I told her, but she'd turned back toward her table. I could tell she still was upset because she was talking under her breath and accenting what she said to her husband with her pointy finger, like he was a kid in trouble. He shook his head in agreement but he kept looking at his plate the whole time as he continued to eat.

"On second thought, you'd better use your forks after all," Uncle Jim said. I think he wanted to prevent more of what my mother calls "unpleasant incidents."

We kept our eyes on our plates for awhile and ate in silence, with forks this time, until Eddo said, "I think I'll use my chop sticks again."

I looked up to say, "You'd better not," and there Eddo sat with a chopstick stuck in each ear.

"Velly good use for chopsticks," Eddo said.

The lady across the aisle did not agree.

"The problem with young people these days is that their parents teach them no manners," she said, glaring right at Uncle Jim. He groaned and covered his eyes with his hands.

"He's not our parent," Eddo said. "We're orphans."

Just then the blonde waitress coming down our aisle with a big tray full of food noticed Eddo's ear chopsticks. Maybe she didn't believe what she saw because her mouth flew open, and she stopped right in her tracks to take another look. The bus boy behind her wasn't watching so he plowed smack dab right into her. The bump caused the food and plates the waitress carried on the tray to keep going right out into thin air, just like Chinese flying saucers, right off the tray.

"Smash! Pop! Crack!" The dishware shattered as the plates fell onto each other and the floor.

What food didn't fly into some of the booths landed in a tangled mess of Egg Chop Mein and Foo Yung Suey littered with pieces of plates. Grease from the fried stuff splattered on the nearby booths.

For a moment it was totally silent while everyone's brains caught up with what just happened.

"Oh, Oh, Oh!" the blonde waitress gurgled while she took two baby steps one way and then two more another way but going nowhere, just like the cars you wind up to cross the floor when they get stopped by the wall or the couch. Her wheels were spinning like that. Finally, she turned around and ran toward the back of the restaurant, wailing, and disappeared through the kitchen door.

What happened next was a bunch of Chinese cussing that I don't know how to write down so I'll just say it sounded like barn owl screeching. I could see the cooks waving their cleavers around in the back through the little window where the waitresses pick up the full plates. The Chinese waitresses waved their arms around and shrieked back at the cooks.

Customers at the tables I could see laughed behind their hands, and looked back and forth from the kitchen to the mess so fast they looked like those dolls with heads on top of springs some people glue to their dashboards.

The cranky lady at the table across from us looked down and saw a mass of soggy noodles like a warm worm nest on her lap. "Ugh!" she huffed, swatting the noodles on the floor with the rest of the mess. She stood up, straightened out her clingy flowered dress with the big, wet spot, swiped at it with a napkin and said to Uncle Jim, "This is beyond acceptable! Harrumph!"

When she said that harrumph part, she shook her head to emphasize and her black, shoulder length hair turned out to be a wig that fell down her forehead onto her nose. She straightened it the best she could with no mirror which wasn't very good because I could see some pink scalp and blobs of gray hair on the left side. She didn't know the napkin got stuck underneath her wig and flapped off to the side. She yelled at her husband, "Follow me, Herbert!" and he did, after wiping his mouth with his napkin. He didn't look at us. He was bald on the top of his head. I guess Mrs. Grouchy was the only one in that family to get a wig. He's the one who really needed one. They tip toed through the mess anyplace there was bare floor and on up to the cash register.

Uncle Jim grabbed the chopsticks out of Eddo's ears. "Just EAT!" he commanded Eddo, "and do NOT use those chopsticks for ANYTHING!" I'll bet he was worried we'd get kicked out of there. That blonde waitress never came back by our table.

Eddo offered to help the bus boy clean up the mess, but he said he reckoned that it would be better all around if Eddo just stayed where he was, so we sat there eating as if nothing out of the ordinary had occurred. Actually, what had happened *was* ordinary if you're around Eddo for very long. The bus boy piled the broken plates up on the tray and scooped the food up with a broom and dust pan. He wiped down the booths with a rag that smelled of bleach, and finally he mopped the aisle clean.

"We need to leave a big tip for the bus boy," I told Uncle Jim.

"That's very nice of you to suggest," Uncle Jim said. "We shall do so."

"I have a dollar," Eddo said, and he dug it out of his pocket and gave it to Uncle Jim.

"Thank you, Eddo. I'm sure he'll appreciate this," Uncle Jim said.

After awhile, when the confusion had died down and people conversed at their tables again, we made up some fun names of our own for Chinese food.

"What would you call a giant plate for hungry eaters?" I asked.

When Eddo and Uncle Jim gave up, I said, "Truck Yuk! Get it? A giant plate—a truck?"

"Boo," Uncle Jim said, but he laughed. Softly, though, so he wouldn't attract attention from the other diners. We'd had enough of that already, thanks to Eddo.

"Here's what I'd name my restaurant," Eddo said. "Kung Food. Get it? And our specialty would be Brown Cow Chow."

I pinched my nose with my fingers and said, "P.U.!" to tease Eddo about his joke and a Chinese waitress arrived with my favorite part of the meal, the fortune cookies.

Eddo's fortune read, "Leave your boat and travel on firm ground."

"I don't even have a boat," Eddo said. "That's dumb."

"That means you should not take so many risks, Eddo," Uncle Jim told him. "See, that's the way fortunes are. They never say anything right out and the fun part is that you have to figure out what they mean."

"It's probably talking about how you ride your bike like a maniac, Eddo," I said. "Every time you race down Sixth Street Hill, it scares me to death."

I refuse to go down Sixth Street Hill because it is straight down. Just looking down from the top of it makes my heart beat right in my mouth so hard I can barely swallow. Anyway, Mom makes me get off and walk my bike down it. It's one time I don't mind minding her.

"Gosh, you sound just like a wimp," Eddo said.

"I am not a wimp, Eddo Richards, and you know it. I just don't want to be a squashed piece of meat all over the street like you're gonna be someday!"

"Let's see what my fortune says," Uncle Jim interrupted, and it was a good thing because I was not using my inside voice. "'Good news from afar can bring you a welcome visitor.' That must mean that Trixie gets to come home with me again. What about yours, Sally Jo?"

"Mine says, 'You'll know exactly what to do at right time to get to the heart of matters.'"

"Sounds romantic to me," Uncle Jim said.

"Oh, yuck," I said.

"Beef or pork?" Eddo said, and we all laughed. I forgot to be mad at him. I grabbed up the fortunes when we left and stuck them in my pocket. I was going to save them and see if any of them came true.

Sally Jo's assignment for her future kids:

Choose one:

Describe everything that is under your bed and why it is there. If you have a good "under the bed" story, tell it.

Tell about a fortune you got once that didn't make sense but later on it came true.

Make up a fortune to put in a fortune cookie. You could even make a batch of cookies and put the fortune in one of them and then whoever got the fortune it would come true for.

ENTRY THIRTEEN, 10/24/83: THE ATTACK OF THE THESAURUS

On the way home Saturday night, full of barbecued pork and sweet and sour spareribs, Eddo and I sat in the back seat making up more weird names for food.

"Know what it's called when my mom accidentally drops an egg when she's cooking breakfast?"

"What?" Eddo said.

"That's 'egg foo gooey.'"

We exploded in copious laughter. That's another way to say we laughed a lot, but Mom won't let me say, "a lot." She says that phrase is overused and there are plenty of other words that can be used in its place. In fact, "plenty" is one of those words. So are "plethora," "myriad," "profusion," and "hordes."

Having a high school English teacher for a mother is a pain and I'm not even in high school yet! She says words are like bait in the sea of knowledge and you won't catch any ideas unless you know lots of words and can use them and recognize them in what you read. Sometimes I don't feel like fishing, if you know what I mean, but I keep a thesaurus around anyway. A dictionary, too.

I wonder if my mom has been teaching her theory to Mr. Wilson because of our English assignment today. He assigned us an exercise using the thesaurus.

Melvin Porter asked, "How come we are studying dinosaurs when that is second grade stuff?"

Everybody laughed.

"Class, quiet down, please," Mr. Wilson said. "We all remember that a thesaurus is not a kind of dinosaur. A thesaurus is a dictionary of synonyms and antonyms which helps us be precise in our writing."

"I knew that," Melvin said, but his red face proved otherwise.

"You will need your dictionaries as well," Mr. Wilson said. After much scrambling and scruffling noises while we prepared ourselves, he said, "Take off one of your shoes. Notice it carefully and then write five words to describe it."

Then we had to find synonyms for those five words and write a poem about our shoes using those five words.

Parts of the classroom, especially where boys sat, began to smell like sweaty, unwashed feet. Eddo showed me his paper when he finished, and I showed him mine.

Eddo found some great synonyms for "moldy," like "gamy," "putrid," "mildew," "stale," and "timeworn." When he looked up "hole" because his shoes are full of them, he found "perforation," "puncture," and "black hole." A black hole is where his shoes should be thrown because of the stench. You can find *that* word under "stink."

This was my poem. See if you can figure out what words I replaced:

> Ankle-*elevated*
> *Saffron* flash
> That pounds cement
> With *vanilla* soles

And *licorice* laces
Visage of Mickey Mouse
Fun on the Run.

I found a lot of food-related words. Maybe that's because we were doing this assignment before lunch and I was hungry.

We didn't put our names on our papers because Mr. Wilson shuffled them around, passed them out again, and we got someone else's to read. Then we tried to guess whose it was. Everyone knew Eddo's because of "putrid," etc. No one else has such stinky, holey, old black shoes. His poem ended, "You are sweet and cover my feet." Only Eddo would call his shoes sweet. Yuck!

Everyone knew mine, too, because I'm the only one with yellow Mickey Mouse shoes. They understood my poem right away.

The poem I received to read said,
"Oh tightly *raddled*
Substantial,
Elongated, alabaster and *ruby*
Footwear of Athena,
Transport me to her heart."

I read it out loud but when Mr. Wilson asked for someone to tell him what it meant, the room was silent.

"I guess we'll just have to look up the words to find out what it means," Mr. Wilson said. (I think that was his devious plan in the first place.) "Please write them on the board for us, Sally Jo," he requested, and I did. The room got quiet except for the ruffling of the thin paper pages of our dictionaries. Lisa was the first to finish and figure out what it all meant.

"Oh, how romantic! It's a love poem," she said.

"Hands!" Mr. Wilson reminded. I wonder if anyone has counted how many times he has to do that.

Leave it to Lisa to decide the poem was a love poem. She turned and smiled at Roger. I just know she thought he wrote it.

"Are we all ready, then?" When nobody said no and some people said yes, Mr. Wilson asked, "What does 'raddled' mean?"

Roger shouted, " 'Laced!' What a weird word. I never heard of that before."

"Thank you, Roger," Mr. Wilson said. "There are many words all of us have never heard of. And next time please remember to raise your hand."

"My mother says even if they sound weird at first, we need to learn new words and use them," I said. "Oops," I said and then raised my hand.

"Ahem, yes, that's very true. I believe . . . I heard . . . her say . . . " Mr. Wilson quit talking and cleared his throat. At the mention of Mom, he looked out the window and got glazy-eyed, like he lost his place. He got a smile on his face and he hugged himself. He stayed like that for at least a minute. I turned around and did a quick survey of our classroom and everyone was staring at him. We didn't know what was going on or what was coming next.

"Uhm, thank you, Sally Jo," he finally said, shaking himself back into the present. "Now, where were we?"

We were here all the time but I sure don't know where he was. Eeuw, what if he was thinking about my mother? Yuck! Oh, my gosh! I just realized his face looked the same as those women on the cover of Eddo's mom's romance novels. If he threw his arms back and if he had long hair and boobs, he would look just like them, all lovey-dovey. Gross!

"Exactly what were we doing?" he asked.

"Can I do 'alabaster' and 'ruby'?" Cindy asked, remembering to raise her hand.

"Oh, yes, certainly," Mr. Wilson said, back on track again. "Be my guest."

"'Alabaster' means white, and 'ruby' is red," Cindy said.

"Right," Mr. Wilson said. He was back to his old self again.

"My mom's name is Ruby," Cindy blurted, without raising her hand.

"Is she red?" Eddo said, not raising his hand either, and everyone laughed.

"Mr. Richards," Mr. Wilson said to Eddo, "since you're so eager to talk perhaps you can tell us what 'elongated' means?"

Eddo was embarrassed because we all knew that Mr. Wilson called us Mr. or Miss when he did not appreciate our behavior. I guess he forgot about Cindy's blurt.

"'Elongated' means long," Eddo said.

"Correct. And who can tell me what 'substantial' means?"

"I can, I can." Shirley waved her hand back and forth.

"Yes, Shirley?" Mr. Wilson said.

"Large," she said and someone snickered, probably because Shirley is HUGE, like The Hulk. Substantial Shirley.

"Right, Shirley. Now, how about 'footwear of Athena'? We know that since we're describing shoes that 'footwear' means shoes, but how does 'Athena' fit in?"

Silence. No one knew.

"I have a suggestion," Mr. Wilson finally said. "How about listing some names of shoes and then we'll look them up and see if any of them are in the dictionary or if the definitions mention Athena."

We listed Avia, New Balance, Nike, Keds. The flipping of dictionary pages began again.

"Oooh, oooh, oooh," Roger said, raising his hand. I was amazed he remembered.

"Roger?" Mr. Wilson said.

"'Nike' means 'Athena, as giver of victory,'" Roger said.

"Let's see who is wearing red and white Nikes, and we'll know who wrote the poem," Lisa said. I could *so* tell she was still hoping Roger had written the poem for her.

Unfortunately for me, the poet was not Roger.

It didn't take too long before we discovered who did write that poem. His face was as red as his shoes. He stared straight down with his nose about one inch away from his desk.

"Ohhhh, Sally Jo!" Lisa crooned when she discovered who the author of the poem was. Everyone stared at me and *my* face got red.

The lunch bell was taking a long time to ring and Mr. Wilson wasn't doing his job of making people turn around and pay attention to him either.

Why did this have to happen to me? Why did I have to pick *this* poem to read? You guessed it. You know who wrote it.

Melvin Porter.

Sally Jo's assignment for her future kids:

Write your name vertically. That means in a straight line from top to bottom. Like

S

A

L

L

Y

Then for each letter of your name, use your thesaurus and dictionary to find an adjective that describes you. For example:

S=sleek

A=adolescent

L=lanky

L=lean

Y=youthful

Etc.

ENTRY FOURTEEN, 10/24/83: JEALOUSY STRIKES

The rest of the school day faded into oblivion. If you don't know that word, look it up.

"How come Melvin is so in love with you, Sally Jo?" Eddo asked when we were walking home.

"He's not in love with me, Eddo." The thought of that made me sick to my stomach. "If you say that again, I'm gonna get mad."

"Well, he's always looking at you and writing things about you. Like, 'Transport me to her heart.'"

"So what? You look at me all the time. You're looking at me now. Are you in love with me?"

Eddo was strangely silent and he stared straight ahead and off to his left, but not at me.

I figured it was the silent treatment, like when Mom gets too mad to yell, so I kept on talking. "Besides, Eddo, who says he wrote that poem to me? There are twelve other girls in the room. Or maybe it's for someone at his other school."

"Oh, come on, Sally Jo. Everyone knows the poem was for you, especially after he kissed you in front of everyone."

"Look, Eddo, I didn't ask him to do that. I don't know why he does that stuff. I told him to cut it out or else. Why do you care?"

The silent treatment again. Eddo still wouldn't look at me.

"Mom says some people just can't help liking another person," I said.

"I'd like to help him help it," Eddo mumbled, and made a jabbing motion with his arm like a boxer.

"What?" I said. I stopped walking. I wasn't sure I heard him right.

"Nothing!" Eddo shouted.

"I just wish he'd leave me alone," I said.

"Me, too," Eddo shouted and sped up so he was way in front of me.

I told Mom about that at bedtime when she came in to say goodnight. "Why would he just walk off when he knows I can't make Melvin stop? Why was he so grouchy?"

"Oh, Honey," Mom said, pushing my bangs out of my eyes. She kept her cool fingertips on my warm forehead for awhile and they felt good. That is a mom technique I am going to remember for when I'm a mom. "It sounds to me like he's jealous. He's had you since the fourth grade all to himself and now all of a sudden there's another contender."

"Contender?" What the heck did that mean?

"Competition. For your attention, for your heart. He's just jealous," Mom explained. "Melvin coming along makes Eddo realize how much he really likes you. And how much he doesn't want to share you."

"But, Mom," I said, "we're just friends. Not girlfriend and boyfriend. Just friends."

She smiled. "Maybe to you. Maybe not to Eddo, though."

She turned off the light. But I was in the dark way before that.

Sally Jo's assignment for her future kids:

Write about a time when someone was jealous of you. Tell what they did and said and how that made you feel.

ENTRY FIFTEEN, 10/31/83: HALLOWEEN

I love running and jumping in crunchy leaves in the fall, and the smoky smell of wood-burning stoves and biting into caramel apples. Fall is full of holidays, too. Halloween and Thanksgiving and Christmas all arrive in three months' time.

Mr. Wilson started off the Halloween festivities by reading Washington Irving's story "The Legend of Sleepy Hollow" to us. The part describing Ichabod Crane, the teacher, sounded just like Melvin Porter to me, tall and skinny with hands dangling a mile out of his sleeves and huge ears. I'll just bet the kids at Crane's school called him "Icky" even though Washington Irving didn't write that down. Maybe the kids at Melvin's old school called him "Icky," too.

I don't blame Icky for disappearing. First his girlfriend said she wouldn't marry him and then some headless horseman chased him and threw his head at him. The highway probably looked pretty good to him by then, in comparison to his life.

On Halloween at our school, kids in grades one through five parade all around the school in their costumes and past the sixth graders who judge them and pick out the best ones—the most original, the prettiest, the ugliest, and whatever other categories we can make up so kids feel good about their costumes. We wear costumes, too, of course. I was going to be Medusa, the lady with snakes for hair, despite my snake phobia, but Mom put her foot down. I could have attached a mop to my head and pretended the fat strings were snakes. I don't see how that could scare Mom in any way, but she has a snake phobia worse than mine, so that's that.

I decided to be a bum with a mustache and a red handkerchief tied on the end of a pole for my belongings instead. Eddo wore his Sherlock Holmes hat and from his mom's closet a trench coat that was so long I could barely see his feet.

Our school has a party on Halloween night to take the place of trick or treating. That way, parents don't have to worry if their kids are getting run over in the dark or receiving tainted candy or apples with razor blades in them. The PTA runs the party and even the parents dress up. This year Mrs. Dominick dressed up like a princess with a blonde wig and a tiara but she didn't fool me with the white mask over her eyes. I knew who it was because of her big behind.

Our class, Mr. Wilson's, made a haunted house at the end of the gym from a lot of black plastic so it was dark and hard to see inside. We set up scary monster faces that popped up and people howled behind them. We hung skeletons that people going through would have to bump into, and we played a tape of howls and ghoulish sounds. Mom did the witch's cackle. She sounded really scary and I wondered if Mr. Wilson worried she might start to sound like that all the time. We made people stop and touch olives and we said they were eyeballs, and cold spaghetti that we told them was guts. The first and second graders were really scared, but after awhile, they all wanted to go through again.

We borrowed Eddo's mom's big garden tub and filled it up with water and apples so we could bob for apples. Eddo got his glasses wet because he was in the way when Shirley went after her apple. By the time he got through gasping for air, shrieking for a towel, and drying his glasses, no apples were left. His face was not happy.

"Here, Eddo, you can have some of my apple," Shirley purred. "Isn't that romantic?" she asked me.

"It's only fair, Shirley," he told her, "after you knocked me out of the way like a big pig in a trough. It was really my apple to begin with." How can he not know she's bonkers for him?

"Oh, Eddo," she said, all sweet, not even upset with him at all. I might forget my resolve to not hit if some guy called me a pig.

I hope Eddo notices one thing, though. Shirley is acting all lovey-dovey towards him and I'm not yelling at him the way he yells at me about Melvin. That's because Eddo and I are just *friends*.

Here is a poem I wrote about Halloween for the school newspaper. I tried to get it in the shape of a pumpkin so I could draw in the eyes and mouth. Eddo liked it and Uncle Jim says it is the best Halloween poem he's ever read.

THE SCARY PUMPKIN

I had a scary pumpkin but nothing
would it say,
though
I threatened it and bribed it and cajoled it all day.
I even gave it lessons in the proper way to talk, but that stupid old
pumpkin just leered at me and balked. I wanted it to howl and scare

the kids on Halloween, but it just couldn't get the art of speaking
through its bean. Its face was dark and evil, flame flickered
from its eyes, but it never would talk and I don't know

why. No matter now, though, 'cause I made
it into pie!

—by Sally Jo Benedict

Sally Jo's assignment for her future kids:
Tell what you like about the fall season.
Describe your favorite Halloween costume.

ENTRY SIXTEEN, 11/10/83: KIDS SAY CUTE THINGS

Today Mom and I went to visit Mrs. Richards because I had a journalistic purpose.

"What was the cutest thing Eddo ever said?" I asked Mrs. Richards, because Eddo and I are writing a column for our school paper about the cute things people said when they were little kids.

Mrs. Richards answered me with this story about Eddo.

"When Eddo got his first wallet, he couldn't wait to fill out his ID card. I told him no, to wait, because we were in the pickup on the way to Grandma's for the weekend and his handwriting would be jerky. But I couldn't stop him because I had to keep my hands on the wheel, so he did it anyway.

"Then he said, 'This is really stupid!' I asked him what he was talking about, and he said, 'This identification card.' So I asked him why," Mrs. Richards told me, and he said, "'Well, here it has a blank to fill in for eyes. Doesn't everyone have two?'"

"I explained that he was supposed to write the *color* of his eyes in the blank, not *how many* eyes he had. I also pointed out that his ID card was a sloppy mess because of riding in the bouncy pickup—just as I had warned."

Eddo hates it when his mom is right like that.

"It's not easy to raise a son," Mrs. Richards said to my mom, who had come along with me to the interview in Mrs. Richards' kitchen. "I never know what he's going to say next."

Then she told me about the time the waitress asked, "How do you want your egg?" and Eddo said, "Cooked."

My mom told Mrs. Richards' the cutest thing I ever said was when I was a baby and got sick. I threw up but I didn't know what it was so I got scared and said, "Mommy, I'm spilling, I'm spilling."

Mrs. Richards laughed.

"Mom, please be quiet. I am trying to conduct an interview," I said.

Mom writes stuff down and keeps it in my baby book, along with a curl of my baby hair and my baby teeth she took when she pretended to be the tooth fairy.

"Oh, sorry," she said.

"Do you have more stories about Eddo?" I asked Mrs. Richards.

"Oh, my, yes," she said, and laughed. "The dentist had to take out all of Eddo's baby teeth because they wouldn't come out by themselves so he never got any money for them. His dad said since the dentist took out his teeth, he couldn't expect the tooth fairy to pay for all that at once. Boy, was Eddo mad, but not for long. I felt so sorry for him that I sneaked in his room when I thought he was sleeping and put some money in his new wallet. He seemed to feel better after that."

He kept those baby teeth in little boxes, but he lost one of the boxes once when he took it to show to his Grandma and he cried for two days like the time he forgot his blankie at day care.

(Mrs. Richards told me that story, too, but I will not put that in our paper.)

This was way before I knew Eddo. I don't think we should have to be responsible for things we do before the age of nine. And I don't think parents should tell other people stories about us either without our permission.

I thanked Mrs. Richards for the interview the way we're supposed to and I left. Mom stayed there, probably to talk about Chet. I don't know how their date turned out besides "Very nice," which was what Mom said when I asked her. I'll bet Mrs. Richards will get to know more about the date than I do.

———————

Sally Jo's assignment for her future kids:

Write about the cute things you said when you were younger than you are now. If you don't know any, ask your mom or grandma.

ENTRY SEVENTEEN, 11/24/83: THANKSGIVING

After Halloween, you just get over eating too much candy and then comes another eating holiday, Thanksgiving. For dinner Mom and I invited Uncle Jim, Eddo and his parents, and Mr. Wilson (whom everyone else calls "Chet" except me and Eddo because we are used to calling him Mr. Wilson).

I set the table and made some turkeys for a centerpiece out of pine cones, pipe cleaners, and construction paper. Mom was cooking and I thought about starving people the way I do every Thanksgiving since the fourth grade. That's because Mom and I ate only one bowl of rice each the whole day so we could see what it was like for some people. For them, our bowl would have been a feast. We gave what we would have spent on food to a world hunger fund. After that, I am always thankful for food, every day.

Just then the doorbell rang and pounding began on the front door. Who knew we'd have a Thanksgiving Day adventure?

Mom came out of the kitchen. "What the . . . ?"

I jumped up and opened the door to see our neighbor Mrs. Biggs, still in her nightgown and bathrobe, her hair sticking out like a toilet brush all over her head. Her eyes were rimmed with red and swollen.

"Have you seen Maryanne?" she sobbed.

Mom opened the screen door. "No, why? What's happened?" Mom sounded worried now. She motioned for Mrs. Biggs to come in, and gave her a big hug.

"Honey, what is it?"

"When I went in this morning to wake Maryanne up for breakfast, she wasn't there. I just thought she was teasing me, so I looked under the bed and in the closet and behind the toybox. Then I felt her cold bed. She hadn't been in it for a long time."

"Did she leave a note?" I asked.

Mom looked at me like I was crazy.

"So I forget she's only four," I said. "Geez. I thought maybe she left some telltale scribbles. She does have paper and crayons, you know."

I knew that because sometimes I stayed with Maryanne when Mrs. Biggs went shopping and Maryanne stayed at our house a couple of months ago when Mrs. Biggs went to the hospital to have their new baby, Kenny. Some people call it baby-sitting, but I call it "staying with" because Maryanne is not a baby. But Mrs. Biggs and Mom weren't listening to me.

"Hank and I searched the whole house and she's nowhere to be found. Just nowhere."

"Did you call the police yet?" Mom asked.

"They make you wait 24 hours before they do anything. I saw it on TV," I said.

Mom shot me one of her warning looks to SHUT UP.

"We hoped she'd come over to play with Sally Jo." Mrs. Biggs sniffled and wiped at her wet cheeks with a crumply Kleenex.

Coloring and playing dolls is not my idea of fun. I only play dolls if I get paid for it. But I didn't say that out loud. I'd gotten my quota of warning looks already.

"If we see her, we'll let you know," Mom said. "I hope you find her soon. As soon as I get the turkey in the oven, I'll go dress and get some people out to scout the neighborhood."

"Thank you," Mrs. Biggs said, and ran across the lawn to her front porch.

"Now what would possess Maryanne to run away, do you suppose?" Mom asked.

I recognized that as one of those questions adults ask when they don't really want an answer but they want to think about the question or they want you to think about it. It's one of those questions like, "How many times have I told you not to do that?" and if you answer and say, "Seven, I think," you get the scrunched-mouth, bug-eyed stare, and sent to your room.

"I'm going over to Eddo's for awhile," I said, and raced out the door before Mom could tell me how not to act around parents whose kids are missing. Even though I'm pretty sure why Maryanne ran away, I didn't say anything in case Mom kept up with her YOU'D BETTER WATCH OUT looks. Sometimes it works better to just do something and then say sorry afterwards. I had an idea of what to do to help out and Eddo would love another Sherlock Holmes adventure.

Eddo was in his pajamas eating toast and peanut butter when I got there. His house smelled like Thanksgiving food, too. I told him what had happened.

"Mumphf! Gurit!" he mumbled, and pieces of chewed toast fell out of his mouth.

"Gross! Don't talk with your mouth full. You look like Godzilla eating monster mash. What did you say?"

He leaped up and ran upstairs. "Be back in a second!"

He returned carrying an old magnifying glass his father had given him and wearing that old Sherlock Holmes hat that he got when he was a kid in third grade. That's why his dad gave him the magnifying glass, so he could pretend to be a famous detective. He mainly looked at ants and eyeballs instead of solving crimes.

"Why do you have your hat and glass?"

"Clues. You never can tell when we might find some good ones."

"Eddo, all we need for my plan is Duke. I'd use Trixie but she's out at Uncle Jim's. He's bringing her back today. Now let's go get Duke out of the back yard."

He looked like those pictures I've seen of Humpty Dumpty wearing a little hat on his fat egg head. We left a note for his parents so they wouldn't think he ran away too, and we left.

"Now here's my plan," I told him again. I'd seen plenty of police television shows and I knew just what we could do. "We'll get something of Maryanne's, like a shoe or a toy, and we let Duke smell it. Then he follows her scent and leads us right to her. What d'ya think?"

"Duke's not a bloodhound, but he's smart. He sniffs things out, but it's usually dead things and poop."

"We'll never know until we try."

We headed over to the Biggs' house to find something in the sandbox we could have Duke smell.

"Any ideas about why she ran away?" Eddo asked me.

"I think it's because of her little brother, Kenny. One time when I stayed with her, she asked if she could stay at our house all the time because her mom and dad didn't love her anymore.

They let Kenny sleep in their room and they held him all the time. She told her parents to take the baby back, but they didn't, so Maryanne was mad."

We took Duke straight to the sandbox in Maryanne's yard and held her dump truck and a naked rubber doll with most of its hair missing and an old, moldy tennis shoe right up to his nose. He didn't like smelling that shoe, I can tell you; in fact, he barked at it and growled and shook it around in his teeth.

"Does he know what he's supposed to be doing?" I asked Eddo. Duke is sweet, but sometimes he's real dumb.

"Lassie always knew what to do."

"Life isn't always like on TV," I reminded him. I began to doubt my own plan.

"Shoot, you're just like Dad with the lecture. Trying Duke out is worth it, especially if we actually find Maryanne. Sherlock Eddo and Duke Watson to the rescue!"

While I watched Duke and the shoe and thought about whether we should have him smell other stuff, he lifted his leg.

"No, Duke!" Eddo said, and Mr. Biggs slammed out his front door yelling. "Get that goshdarn dog out of here!" (He did not say "goshdarn" but I am not going to write the word he did say because Mom might find my journal and I don't want her to have a snit fit about my language.) Besides, my future kids are going to be reading this.

"But Mr. Biggs, we're just . . . " I began to explain.

"I don't care what you're doing, I don't want dog pee in that sandbox. I have enough to worry about without having to buy new sand."

Duke whined. He doesn't like yelling. He took off scampering for the front hedges and relief.

"I think Duke's smelled enough," Eddo said.

"Smart thinking," I said and we ran to follow Duke.

When I got to the street, I turned around, and Mr. Biggs stood over by the sandbox holding the moldy shoe in his hand, crying.

First, we went to the park and Duke ran to the boat landing on the river because he loves the water. A fisherman was putting his boat in the water and his wife who had her hair in curlers was just getting in it. Duke splashed out into the water and tried to get in the boat, too. The boat rocked and tipped suddenly and the lady wasn't ready and she fell over into the water.

"Aiiiiie!" she screamed, like a rusty siren.

The water isn't deep there so I don't know what she was screaming about, kind of like Eddo in the park pond the first day I met him. Of course, the water was cold.

"Oh, my hair got wet," she wailed, and her husband yelled at Duke, who got the heck out of there, fast. Poor Duke. Two people yelling at him this morning. Eddo put Duke on his chain so he'd get into less mischief.

Maryanne wasn't on the swing sets or the merry-go-round or in the garbage pails. I told Eddo I didn't think she'd be there anyway.

He began inspecting some limp lettuce with his magnifying glass. It hung down all over his hand and runny white stuff dripped off it and down his hand.

"Eddo, we have more important work to do. Limp lettuce is not a clue."

Duke sniffed over by the restrooms. We searched the restrooms inside until some guy got mad at Eddo for looking under his stall door.

"What the hell are you doing?" he shouted.

"I'm looking for a lost girl. She's about four years old."

The guy said, "Well, she *certainly* wouldn't be in *here!*"

"You never can tell, Sir. I had to look just in case. Sorry." Eddo came out of there holding his nose and waving his hand around. I laughed.

"I told you what Duke usually sniffs out," Eddo said.

Duke took off sniffing over by our school, although I didn't think Maryanne even knew what school was. Duke wouldn't go near the cafetorium, though. He whimpered and pulled back on his chain and Eddo couldn't budge him. Duke remembered the punch and the balloons popping and the shouting, I'm pretty sure. I know I did.

Duke sniffed his way downtown and turned around to look at us like he was saying, "Hurry up!" When we got to Safeway which was open until noon, people looked at Eddo like he was crazy. Partly that was because of his dorky hat, and partly because he asked if they'd seen a four year-old girl wearing one moldy tennis shoe.

"Just because you wear your moldy tennis shoes, doesn't mean everyone does," I explained. "That shoe has probably been in the sandbox a long time."

Then Eddo told people he'd lost his little sister. An old lady with blue hair, wearing a flowered dress and a greasy apron patted him on the head. "Poor little fella," she said.

We walked all over town but most places were closed for the holiday. I decided that Duke couldn't find people with his nose, but I didn't want to hurt Eddo's feelings so I said I was starving.

"Could we please go home to get a snack?"

"Yeah, Duke could do better on a full stomach, too."

"It's his nose that doesn't work, Eddo, not his stomach."

"Aw, what do you know? I bet after a snack Duke will find his man."

"It's a girl, Eddo, not a man." I like for people to be precise.

On the way to Eddo's kitchen, we said hi to his mom who was on the living room couch reading another romance novel. The pictures on the front of those books make me laugh. They always show a lady with long, long hair, lying back in a man's arms with her boobs showing and usually the man and woman are kissing or just about to. No one ever really looks like that, in my experience, anyway. Well, except for Mr. Wilson that day in class when I mentioned Mom.

"Why aren't you with Sally Jo's mom looking for Maryanne?" Eddo asked her.

"I scoured the neighborhood as much as I can scour. I had to come home and put my feet up. Now I think it's a job for the authorities. Besides I have rolls in the oven for dinner later and I have to watch them. If you are going to snack, don't eat too much because dinner's not too far away. And do not eat the food I'm taking for dinner."

We got some cheese crackers and took them outside to the backyard by the big tree where Eddo has his treehouse. When he's mad at his mom for throwing away his stinky shoes or making him clean under his bed, that's where he goes. When his mom calls him to come vacuum the house, that's where he hides.

Because we couldn't climb the spindly boards nailed to the tree for steps with our hands full, we both lay back on the lounge chairs that his mom had forgotten to bring in for the winter. Duke ate the treats Eddo gave him in two big gulps. He licked his snout with his tongue and then took a sniffing tour of the yard to make sure everything was the same as the last time he was here. His sniffing is like reading the newspaper and Duke wanted to keep up with events.

Eddo stuck his Sherlock Holmes hat on Duke's head and we laughed. Suddenly, Duke barked up at the tree house. "Grrrrrr!" he said, deep in his throat.

Eddo and I looked at each other. "Maybe there's a bum up there and he's got a knife to kill us, "I whispered.

"Don't be stupid," Eddo whispered back, but I could tell he was scared, too.

"Go up and see what's there," I whispered again.

"Why don't you go up?"

"It's your tree."

"Yeah, but you want to know what's up there."

"Yeah, I do," I said. "If you're too chicken to go up in your own tree, I will."

That got to Eddo. He can't stand to be called chicken or for me to do something he can't.

"OK, OK, I'll go."

He grabbed the bag full of clothespins from the clothesline to bop someone with if he had to. Creeping step by step up the tree house steps, he stopped at each one and looked up at the doorway. He expected to be slaughtered by my imaginary knife man.

Duke kept barking and grrrring at the bottom of the tree.

"Shut up!" I said. If Duke disturbed Mrs. Richards in the middle of a book, he'd be sorry and we might not get any Thanksgiving dinner.

One of the steps was loose on its nail and creaked, spinning downward when Eddo stepped on it. He grabbed onto the next step up with both hands, dropping the clothespin bag and all the clothespins all over the lawn. Boy, would his mom be mad. He moaned behind his clenched teeth. For a few moments he hung there until his feet found a stable step.

"Smooth move. Are you OK?" I asked.

"Of course I'm OK," he said, but his teeth were still clenched.

He climbed the next two steps and disappeared bit by bit into the tree house door.

I felt relief when he poked his head back out and said, "Come on up. It's safe. Just watch that bad step. You won't believe who's up here."

As I stuck my head through the door, before I got used to the dark, Eddo said, "Duke's not so stupid after all."

Then my eyes got adjusted and I saw what he meant.

Yep, Duke was in a class with Lassie all right.

Over in the corner with her arm wrapped around her Raggedy Ann doll was Maryanne, asleep. Next to her was a suitcase and her favorite blankie with blue dolls stitched all over it.

"Shall we wake her up?" Eddo asked. "If she can sleep through Duke barking, she must really be tired."

"Her mom and dad will want to know she's all right, Eddo. I saw her dad crying."

We woke her up and for a minute, she didn't know where she was. Then she cried.

"What's the matter?" I asked her. "How come you're up here in Eddo's tree house?"

"I ran away from home. I live here now."

"You can't live here," Eddo said. "This is just for big kids. You coulda hurt yourself on that loose step."

"I'm a big kid. I'm four years old."

"Why can't you live at home?" I asked her.

"Mommy and Daddy don't like me."

"Oh, they do, too."

"No, sir. They like Kenny now. Daddy said no ice cream."

"Why?" I asked.

"Cause I didn't clean up my toy box. I got dirty clothes. I got in trouble. Mommy says get down out of her lap because I'm a big girl now."

"Well, you are a big girl," I said. "You just said so yourself."

"Mommy says Kenny is so cute. Not me."

"So you got in trouble. Big deal," Eddo said. "Heck, I get in trouble almost every day."

"He does. I can vouch for that," I said.

"I don't like it much either, but that's how you know your parents *do* love you," Eddo told her. "If they didn't love you, they wouldn't say anything to you at all, ever."

Judging from all the lecturing that goes on over at Eddo's house, I guess his parents are crazy about him. I thought that was a good thing for him to say to Maryanne and I told her it was the same at my house. I told her what I knew about babies too. I learned a lot from when my Aunt Susie had twins when I was in the fourth grade and I went to help her out. Those babies never stopped crying or messing their diapers.

"Your mom and dad aren't ignoring you. It's just that babies have to be held all the time, even though they leak," Eddo said.

"Your mom held you all the time when you were a baby, too," I said.

"She did?"

"Sure. Now it's Kenny's turn."

"I think you should go back home now," I said. "Your mom and dad are worried sick about you."

"How do you know?"

"Your mom came over to our house this morning to ask if we'd seen you. And I saw your dad standing in the sandbox holding your shoe and crying."

She thought about that for a minute. Just to clinch the deal, I said to her, "The next time you feel all alone, call me up and we'll play dolls."

I don't know why I said that, knowing how I feel about dolls. It just came out.

"OK," she said, her face brightening. "Let's go."

We packed up her blankie and Raggedy Ann doll in her suitcase and walked her back home. When they saw us coming up the walk, Mr. and Mrs. Biggs rushed out of the house, bumping into each other.

"My baby, my baby," Mrs. Biggs wailed, getting on her knees and grabbing Maryanne.

"Where were you?" Mr. Biggs said.

We said Duke tracked her, that we found her in Eddo's tree house.

"Good Boy," Mr. Biggs said to Duke and patted him on the head. Duke likes that better than getting yelled at. He wagged his tail and sat there like he was part of the conversation.

"Why did you run away?" Mrs. Biggs asked Maryanne.

"You didn't love me. You paid attention to Kenny and not to me."

"I told Maryanne that's the way it always is with babies 'cause they need lots of holding," I said.

"Well, yes they do. Sally Jo is right," Mrs. Biggs told Maryanne. She smiled at me appreciatively.

"Thank you," she mouthed. "And you know what else?" she said to Maryanne. "Since you're such a big girl, you can help hold Kenny, too. How's that?"

Maryanne nodded. "Eddo gets in trouble too. His parents love him a lot."

Mrs. Biggs smiled. She must've heard some stories about Eddo. "I'm sure they do. And we love you, too."

Maryanne hugged her mom and dad.

"How can we ever thank you?" Mr. Biggs said. I'll bet he felt dumb for having yelled at us this morning.

"Glad to help, Sir," Eddo said.

"Yes, thank you Sally Jo and Eddo," Mrs. Biggs said, and she stood up and kissed Eddo on the cheek because he was closest to her. He turned all red and wiped the wet spot off with his shoulder.

"And thanks to Duke, too," she said, "but I won't kiss him."

"Sometimes I wish I was a dog," Eddo said, under his breath.

"Good boy, Duke," Mr. Biggs said again, and stuck out

his hand to pat Duke. Instead, Duke licked his hand all over. Mr. Biggs looked like he didn't know what to do with his sticky dog-spit hand. Then he wiped it on his pants and took hold of Maryanne's hand.

"Remember about dollies, Sally Jo," Maryanne said as she walked off between her parents.

"You betcha," I said, and waved goodbye. Why is it that little kids can't remember where they put their shoes, but they never forget the things you'd like them to?

"Remember about dollies," Eddo mimicked, and I chased him down the street. "See you at dinner!" he shouted as he ran around the corner towards his house.

Our dinner was great. Mom baked the turkey and the dressing. I opened the can of cranberry sauce and the olives. I like to put the big black ones on my fingers and bite them off one by one—the olives, I mean, not my fingers! We had Mrs. Richards' fresh-baked rolls with real butter, not margarine, and green beans and potatoes and gravy and Mr. Wilson's lettuce salad full of tomatoes, cucumbers, carrots, sunflower seeds and honey mustard dressing topped with freshly-ground black pepper.

Uncle Jim prepared baked squash from his farm just the way I like it with brown sugar and marshmallows, and he made three pumpkin pies with whipped cream straight from his cows. Well, the whipped cream didn't come out of the cow that way, but you know that. And I don't know how to make pie so that part of my Halloween poem was a lie.

Of course, Duke and Trixie were here but they stayed in the back yard and I gave them some Thanksgiving dog treats. I made them out of oatmeal, whole wheat flour, natural peanut butter, eggs and chicken broth. To those dogs, my treats were better than turkey.

Mr. Richards spoke up during dinner, and I felt a lecture coming on. "You know, the Pilgrims probably did not feast on turkey at their first Thanksgiving Dinner. Wild turkeys were too hard for them to catch, so they ate EELS instead because the Indians had taught them how to catch eels."

EELS! I felt them sliding down my throat and then shooting right back up again.

"Yuck, Mr. Richards!"

I swallowed a couple of times after hearing that just to make sure everything I'd eaten stayed down there in my stomach. The adults all laughed politely but I noticed they were swallowing too.

Mr. Wilson changed the subject, thank goodness, by suggesting that everyone tell what they were thankful for.

"I am thankful for good friends that allow me to be a part of their families." He looked at my mom and smiled and she smiled back at him. All the adults looked at the both of them and smiled. Nobody looked at me, so I think he should have said "girlfriend" and not just "friends."

I felt invisible, kind of like Maryanne, but just then Uncle Jim said, "I am thankful for my farm and my family, and I'm glad Sally Jo shares Trixie with me." This time everybody's smiles were for me.

We went around the table saying what we were thankful for, and when it was my turn, I said, "I am thankful for Mom and for good friends, too, like Eddo. I'm also glad we don't have to eat eels anymore because I like the idea of turkey a lot better. And I'm thankful Duke found Maryanne today."

"Hear, hear!" the adults said.

"Your adventure had a good ending," Mrs. Richards said. "Eddo, what are you thankful for?"

"I am thankful for my parents, a friend like Sally Jo, Duke, and pumpkin pie," Eddo said.

"That's my cue!" Uncle Jim said, and he served slices of his pumpkin pie with piles of fluffy whipped cream on top.

"Goodness gracious, Tricia," Mr. Richards said, "I think you have been a wonderful hostess and we have just outdone ourselves with this wonderful meal. Good friends, good food and gratitude. What could be better?"

No talk of eels, I thought, or lovey-dovey looks over the mashed potatoes, *that* could be better, but I didn't say anything.

Eddo and I went for a walk with the dogs down by the river. A lot, I mean *a profusion* of people were out walking, too, probably to wear off their dinners. I felt like a stuffed teddy bear with a big, round stomach and short, little arms and legs. Or a balloon full of air. Then I could unplug myself and whip around every which way until I was my empty self again. Eddo and I tooted like emptying balloons. I think the turkey is to blame.

Sally Jo's assignment for her future kids:

Tell five things you are thankful for. Tell about a time you ran away.

ENTRY EIGHTEEN, 12/14/83:
EDDO PEEKS

The first thing Eddo said when he came over this morning was that he found out where his toys were, way back in the dark on the top shelf of the hall closet. Isn't that where presents are always hidden? Hall closets or bedroom closets or under the bed or in the attic. You'd think parents are all mentally defective when it comes to hiding gifts. Why can't they think of better places? Like on an unused shelf at the morgue, for example. Who would ever think of looking there or even wanting to look? Or in the freezer, under the beef roast and packages of peas.

Chances are, you'll find your presents if you really want to. I never want to because I don't like my surprises spoiled and I don't want my mom to say, "OK, then, let's just not have presents like the kids in China and see how that feels."

I guess Eddo can't hold back his curiosity, though. When his mom went to the store, he peeked.

We were sitting on the living room couch eating some Oreos when he told me, "I got a Pac Man video game, Taco's "After Eight" album and Queen's "Greatest Hits" album, a race track with a General Lee car, and a blue and green striped rugby shirt."

Those were all things Eddo had put on his Christmas list. I am glad he got some new albums because I am tired of hearing him sing, "Total Eclipse of My Farts," and humming the "Dukes of Hazzard Theme Song." Now he can tap dance to "Puttin' On The Ritz." He can put on his undershirt and show his pretend muscles and sing, "We Are The Champions" in his own bedroom now and I won't have to see him.

But still, I don't like cheating and I think that's what opening your presents is. That cheats you and your parents both. He's just showing off by telling me about all his presents as if I care one bit.

"I don't like your bragging," I said. "Just think of those kids in China who don't even get one gift."

I secretly wish he'd get caught but I'm not a tattle tale. I won't be able to talk to Mom about this until after Christmas so I'm writing about it in my journal to let off steam. Besides, I realize I'm jealous because no way am I going to get so many things. Mom's teaching salary is at the top of the poverty level which I know because that's how she qualified for the low-income loan so she could buy our house. We don't have much money left after paying bills every month.

"I'm not bragging," Eddo said. "I'm just stating facts."

"Fine," I said. "I'm real happy for you. Now, I have a head-ache, so go home."

"Are you mad at me?" Eddo asked.

"No!" I said, but I was. "I said I have a headache and it's getting worse, so go home."

"Jeesh, bite my head off," Eddo said, and he got up without

looking at me and slammed the front door when he left. That didn't help my headache, even if it was imaginary. There's a reason certain words rhyme, like "annoy" and "boy."

I'm still grouchy. Writing in my journal helped only a little bit. I think I'll go outside and yell in the back yard. Maybe Mr. Mead will come ring his dingy-dingy at me.

———————————

Sally Jo's assignment for her future kids:

Tell about a time when a friend did something that you thought was wrong. What did you want to say to your friend?

ENTRY NINETEEN, 12/19/83: THE NECKLACE

A present came for me in the mail today. I did not tell Eddo about it right away because of what it is and who I think might have sent it. I went out to bring in the mail this afternoon when I got home from school and I found it, a little package addressed to me.

I opened it up and discovered a gold locket shaped like half a heart with a jagged edge so it looks like it has been torn apart. The word "Love" is written vertically down the center. Whoever sent it must have the other half. I can't find any name on the box and the postmark is blurred. Mom doesn't know who sent it either.

We don't think Grandpa and Grandma sent it because we're going there in three days for Christmas, so why would they send something?

"It appears you have a secret admirer," Mom said. "What's the name of that boy at school?"

"Melvin Porter?"

No. Please make it not from him, I thought.

I asked Eddo to come over so I could show it to him and find out if he sent it. He was wearing his dad's red Ace Hardware cap that kept falling down to the bridge of his nose so he had to lift up his head and squint out the bottom part of his glasses. He came into our kitchen and I motioned him over to the table.

"I didn't send it," Eddo said when I showed him the necklace. "Are you going to wear it?"

"Sure. Why not? It's so pretty it seems a waste to leave it in the box just because I don't know who gave it to me."

"I bet I know who did it."

"Who?"

"Who else, Sally Jo? Who else keeps doing stuff like this?"

"Melvin Porter?"

"Yeah, your boyfriend Melvin Porter." Eddo emphasized the word "boyfriend" in a nasty tone and it made me mad. His forehead wore that big "11" that comes between your eyebrows when you're making your eyes mean.

"I get tired of you saying that all the time, Eddo. He's NOT my boyfriend!"

"Oh, yeah? Why don't you just give the necklace back to him, then?"

"How can I give it back to him if I don't know he's the one who gave it to me? And if he's not, I don't want to give him any ideas. If I ignore him, maybe he'll forget about me and leave me alone."

"Fat chance," Eddo said.

"What's your problem, anyway?" I asked. "It's me that Melvin's bugging, not you."

Eddo looked at me like there was something I wasn't getting. He stared at me and made his mouth into a pucker so his breath whooshed in and out.

"Oh, he's bugging me plenty."

"What?"

"Never mind," he said. "I hafta go help my dad paint the kitchen. See you around."

"Yeah, so long," I said, but I knew he was upset. He slammed the front door again on his way out. If he keeps that up, we are going to need new hinges soon.

Why was he so bothered about a stupid necklace? It's not like *he's* my boyfriend.

I fingered the piece of paper that came inside the box, the one I was glad I hadn't shown Eddo. It was typed so I couldn't tell who wrote it and it said, *Wear this next to your heart.*

The necklace didn't have to be from Melvin Porter, did it? Was it so impossible to think someone else might like me? I decided to keep an eye out for clues like someone throwing spit-wads at me in class or running into me on the playground, stuff boys do when they like you.

I put on the necklace and tucked it under my tee-shirt, but not because it was romantic. I hid it only because I didn't want the kids at school or Eddo asking questions before I found out who gave it to me.

You know what? I don't care if it did come from Melvin.

I hate when someone tells me to never mind.

Sally Jo's assignment for her future kids:
Write about a time when a friend got mad at you for nothing.
What things do you not like for people to say to you?

ENTRY TWENTY, 12/25/83: THE CHRISTMAS SURPRISE

We didn't stay home, so Christmas was different for us this year. First, Mom, Uncle Jim, and I went to my Grandma and Grandpa's house in La Grande, Oregon. Second, Mr. Wilson came with us, which surprised me. Third, we rode Amtrak from Portland. Trixie stayed home with Eddo and Duke. I promised Eddo I would phone him every day, but Mom said she'd have to see about that.

On the train we visited with people who mostly wore their winter coats or had them stashed next to them on their seats. I saw families and old people alone and soldiers. One old lady, wearing a gray, wool coat with hairballs, her hair all white and wild, sat stiffly with her black vinyl purse in her lap. Her hands rested on top grasping the brass clasp. She stared out the window and I wondered what she was thinking about. I hoped she was going to have a lot of fun when she got wherever she was going.

I walked through all the cars from front to back. Try walking straight when the train is swaying back and forth and sometimes front and back. When I walked past the teensy bathrooms that seemed barely big enough for me, I wondered how guys would pee and not miss. One big jerk and their aim would be off. Then when I had to use the toilet, I found out they do miss. Yuck!

In the dining car on this train there was a deli with sandwiches, potato chips and pop. We didn't buy any food because Mom packed our lunch for us but we went there to play Scrabble. Mr. Wilson brought his little Spanish guitar, so we sang Christmas carols with the other passengers in our own car. Well, the ones who wanted to. Some grouchy people ignored us.

Mr. Wilson was just like one of our family and I felt happy having him around and people knowing he belonged with us. He even put his arm around me and Mom when we shared a bench seat and it felt normal to me, like friends.

Outside it was snowing. I watched the Columbia River all the way up the gorge to count the barges and boats until we pulled away on the wheatlands. Winding up Cabbage Hill took forever and then, before we knew it, we were pulling into the station with its red-tiled roof in La Grande.

"Oh, look!" Mom exclaimed, and out the window I could see Grandpa and Aunt Susie holding up a banner that said, "Merry Christmas and Welcome: Tricia, Jim, Sally Jo, and Chet!" That got me excited, I can tell you, because all the passengers knew then that we were special and that we had Chet with us.

"Mom, where's Grandma? I can't see her anywhere," I said.

"I don't know, Honey. Maybe she's still in the waiting room, keeping warm."

"Sally Jo, look at Santa Claus," Uncle Jim said.

Sure enough, there was a Santa out there, waving to all the passengers, his breath making little puffs like a mini-steam engine in the cold air. When we got off the train, the

Santa was at the door giving out candy canes to each departing passenger.

"Merry Christmas," he said gruffly when it was my turn to jump down, and he stuck a candy cane in my coat pocket. Yum!

"Boy, Amtrak sure has a good idea with this Santa greeter, don't they?" Mr. Wilson remarked to my uncle.

I ran up to Grandpa and gave him a big hug and he lifted me up into the air. It's a long way to the top of him.

"My gosh, Sally Jo! I can barely lift you anymore. You are really growing!" Grandpa exclaimed as he set me back down on the ground.

"She truly is," Mom said. "Hope you didn't get a hernia. She's quite the young lady."

"What's a hernia?" I asked.

"You don't want to know," Grandpa said.

I did want to know but I decided to look up "hernia" in Grandma's dictionary later.

Next I hugged Aunt Susie and I said, "Where's Grandma?"

"Oh, she stayed home with the twins to bake cookies," she said, pushing her curly blond hair out of her eyes.

Aunt Susie has twin boys who are four years old and never stand still so I knew Grandma would be taking a nap after they went home.

Then I noticed that all the other passengers had gone inside the warm Spanish-styled station, but Santa was hanging around us. Everyone started hugging Santa, and I wondered why. It was freezing out. Ice was everywhere underfoot, my nose hairs were freezing together, and icicles hung like daggers from the roof. If Eddo had been here, he would have played pirates with them.

Why did some Santa care about our family anyway? Wasn't he cold? I knew I was.

Santa walked over to me and when he hugged me, I saw everyone smiling and looking at me.

"What are you looking at?" I said, because I felt strange with everyone staring.

"Look at Santa," Uncle Jim said, and when I did, Santa pulled down his beard, and guess who it was. My Grandma!

"Oh!" I screamed. "GRANDMA!" and I hugged her good. "You really fooled me. This was the best Christmas surprise ever!"

Everyone laughed and hugged all over again, and then we headed for the cars because the wind had blown the snow on us so we all looked like snowmen.

Aunt Susie went home to her house where the twins really were, keeping Uncle Dwight company. We forded snowdrifts in order to reach Grandma and Grandpa's one-story farmhouse. Opening the door to the back porch where the woodbox and the washer and dryer are, I felt a blast of warm air full of baking smells. When we got settled and sat around the kitchen bar in Grandma's giant kitchen, we had hot chocolate, Christmas sugar cookies and cinnamon rolls. The wood fires in the kitchen stove and the living room stove warmed us up.

"Come on, Sally Jo," Grandpa said. "Let's go out and pack in some wood."

I put on Grandma's boots which were way too long, and her coat and gloves and helped him stack firewood in the porch bin, enough to hold us all night.

Grandpa has to go out every summer and cut down trees and make them into the right size for his stoves and then stack them all. With all the chores to do on the farm, I'm sure that's why he's so skinny. Grandma too. They are always busy.

Grandma took a nap like I predicted. When she woke up, I helped her fix dinner. After the dishes were done and Aunt Susie came back to visit, Grandpa had an idea.

"How about a little music?" he asked Mr. Wilson.

"I'm up for that," Mr. Wilson said. He played his guitar and Grandpa played his harmonica. Every once in awhile, Grandpa hit his harmonica on his leg to shake out the spit. Our family loves music. We must have sung almost every song ever written, not just Christmas ones.

Mr. Wilson even knew Grandpa's old songs like "Red River Valley" and "Turkey in the Straw." Aunt Susie, who had brought her guitar with her, sang several love songs that she sings with her band, Crinoline. Uncle Jim sang "Old Time Rock 'n' Roll" and everyone jumped up and danced, even Grandma and Grandpa. It's a good thing Grandma had a nap so she'd have enough energy. I wished Eddo could've been here.

That night after Aunt Susie went home, I hugged everyone again, and Mom tucked me into bed up in the white attic dorm room, full of twin beds for all the grandkids who were always coming to visit. Mom had to stay in the middle part of the room where the ceiling was the highest because the roof sloped down on each side. I had one of Grandma's quilts over me, with all kinds of green and white material and little girls with green bonnets in every square.

"Grandma's surprise was super! Don't we have a great family?" I said to Mom.

"Yes, we do, Sally Jo."

"I love Grandma's great cinnamon rolls. They're my favorite, like Heaven made out of yeast and flour and sugar."

"Is that what you liked best at dinner tonight?"

"Yes, and I liked all the singing. Mr. Wilson knew all of our songs, too. I think Grandma and Grandpa like him. Grandma kept giving him cookies all night long."

"Sally Jo, how do *you* feel about Chet?"

"He plays guitar good . . . "

"Well," Mom corrected.

" . . . well, and he's a good teacher. I am glad he came with us for Christmas. He feels like family now."

"That's good," Mom said.

"But I feel dumb calling him Chet. I'll try if you want me to, though."

"Whatever you feel comfortable with. I don't want to push you into anything. Besides, you should talk it over with him."

"Do you think Mr . . . uh . . . Chet likes *us*, Mom? You and me, too?"

"That's a distinct possibility." She smiled when she said that.

"I'm glad he came with us," I said again.

"I'm glad too," Mom said. "I like him very much." She got that dopey romance novel look but her shirt was buttoned up so no boobs showed. She stared out the window even though it was dark outside. Then she turned to me and said, "And I love my little sweetie very much."

"I love you, too, Mom."

"Sleep tight and don't let the bedbugs bite."

"Nighty-night, Mom. Merry Christmas."

"Merry Christmas, Honey."

You know, I didn't even feel cold out in the snow when everybody was hugging. Even when I hugged Mr. Wilson and he hugged me on the train, it seemed natural. Maybe that's what people mean when they say love is a warm feeling. When somebody loves you, that makes you feel special, like I felt when I saw the banner out the train window.

I'll bet all our love is why Mr. Wilson likes being around our family. I need to ask Mom if she loves Mr. Wilson but after our long day, I'm too tired right now. This Christmas is going to be a good memory.

I thought about Trixie and hoped she was all right with Eddo, and then I thought about the fights Eddo and I'd been having which wasn't a good memory and then I fell asleep.

———————

Sally Jo's assignment for her future kids:
   Tell your best Christmas memory ever.

ENTRY TWENTY-ONE, 12/26/83: REPRISAL

"Hi, Eddo. How is Trixie and how are you?"

"Trixie is OK, but I'm not. I didn't have a good Christmas."

"How come? And talk fast before Mom yells at me to get off the phone." Grandma's ugly gold phone with finger smudges all over was short and squat and the numbers in the dial were almost worn off. The earpiece was sticky on my ear.

I guess Eddo hadn't put the packages back the way he found them. Somehow Mrs. Richards knew he had been into the packages and she did something about it. She didn't yell at him or accuse him of anything, like Mom would have. She did something else instead.

"When I opened my presents yesterday, all I got were handkerchiefs, undershorts, and socks."

"Where did all that other stuff go?"

"I don't know," he said, and he started crying, right there on the phone. I didn't know what to say and I almost cried myself, even though he deserved what he got.

"I got a Walkman and a Michael Jackson *Thriller* tape, a green sweatshirt with a hood and little round, solid-gold earrings."

"Wow. Nice, Sally Jo." His voice didn't sound very wow-y.

"Get off the phone, Sally Jo," Mom yelled.

"I'm sorry, Eddo. My mom's yelling at me so I have to go. I hope things get better."

I'll bet Eddo won't ever peek at his presents again. I'll bet when he grows up to be a father, he'll think of a much better hiding place for presents than the hall closet. No, I don't think Christmas this year was as good a memory for Eddo as it was for me.

———————————

Sally Jo's assignment for her future kids:

Write about a time when you were disappointed with your Christmas presents for some reason.

ENTRY TWENTY-TWO, 01/27/84: JANUARY DEPRESSION

After the excitement of Christmas, January is so dull. The earth and the sky blend to form a world of gray. Nothing is left to celebrate, nothing is growing outside, not even in Mr. Mead's yard. He doesn't even turn on his Malibu lights. Rain, snow and wind spit all over us. We get up in the dark and come home from school in the dark. What makes it even worse is that January is five weeks long. Mom is super glad for payday at the end of January because we always run out of money. I think a year of Januarys would make people go crazy.

Eddo hasn't come over this whole month since the day I got back and went to get Trixie.

"Thanks, Eddo," I said. "She looks happy so I think you took good care of her."

"You're welcome," he said.

"Thank you for the Alfred Hitchcock mystery book," I said.

"You're welcome," he said.

"How are you today?" I asked, because he didn't look as happy as Trixie.

"My parents must have figured I'd learned my lesson."

"Why?"

"They brought out my real presents finally."

"That's cool then, isn't it?"

"It's just not the same. Those things don't seem half so neat after what I've been through."

"Sorry," I said.

"Yeah," he said.

That was the end of December.

January got even worse and I don't mean the weather.

A week after we got back, I called him up to hang out, and he said, "Why don't you call up your *boyfriend*, Melvin Porter?"

I slammed the phone down, I was so mad. I saw him coming out of Ms. Montgomery's office the next day. I don't know why he went and I don't care. I hope she told him to quit being such a brat.

I waited until now, the end of the month, to even write in my journal in case something good happened, but it hasn't. I guess he's still miffed at the end of January about what happened at Christmas with his gifts and about the necklace.

I have to take Trixie for a walk every day when I get home from school. After our walk, we build a fire and curl up in front of it and stare into the flames and think about better times. When she's asleep and dreaming, her legs move and I suppose she's thinking about running around in Uncle Jim's fields or down at the river with Duke.

Mr. Wilson came over to our house when Uncle Jim came for a visit, so we all played Scrabble. We always have fun doing that, but it wasn't the same without Eddo here. When I made the word "necklace," I didn't want to play anymore.

The only holiday in January is Martin Luther King Day.

Mr. Wilson read us the speech, "I Have A Dream," and then we had to write about our dreams. Eddo started writing about a four-headed monster, but Mr. Wilson, who was walking around looking at our work put a stop to that.

"A four-headed monster is a nightmare, not a dream, Mr. Richards. By 'dream' Mr. King meant a goal for the future, something that you hope will happen in your lifetime that you can be a part of."

We read our dreams the next day in front of the all-school assembly honoring Mr. King. Many kids wrote about no more nuclear weapons and no more war.

"I hope people can just get along and not have any fights or wars," I said when it was my turn. My goal was for Eddo to hear it and get the message.

"I would like to be a famous actress with lots of boyfriends and send money to starving children all over the world," Lisa said.

"I want to be a pro football linebacker and own a pizza parlour and make pineapple and Canadian bacon pizza," Roger said.

"I dream of having a lot of friends, one very special girl in particular," Melvin Porter said.

I got my evil eye look ready for Eddo in case he made a big deal about Melvin's dream. When I peeked over my right shoulder two levels up on the bleachers, I saw Eddo all hunched over staring at his shoes like he never even heard a word.

Because her mom took photos of the event, Lisa and Roger standing next to Mr. Ellis got their picture in our town's weekly newspaper. Mr. Ellis is still our principal despite Lisa's mom's big fuss about his head ending up in her lap at the dance last Fall. Mr. Wilson was in the picture, too.

Since I had a bunch of free time thanks to Eddo, I either went over to Cindy's after school or she came over to my house.

One time when we came downstairs for a snack and something to drink, we saw Mr. Wilson and my mom kissing on the couch.

"Don't look!" I told Cindy, but I think she saw anyway.

"Oh, hi, Sally Jo, Cindy," Mr. Wilson said, just like nothing had happened.

"Hi." I pushed Cindy into the kitchen.

I felt stupid that they saw me while they were kissing and that I saw them. Now I couldn't deny to myself that they actually kissed or that Mom might be falling in love.

"Is your mom going to marry Mr. Wilson?" Cindy asked me, in her normal voice, which sounds like those guys that yell in their commercials about the cars they are selling.

"Shh!" I whispered. "I don't know."

"It's weird seeing them kiss, huh?" Cindy asked, whispering, too.

I had never thought about my Mom marrying Mr. Wilson. That would make him my dad, a step-dad, I guess, and I already had a dad once. Wouldn't a step-dad boss me around? I don't know if I want to get bossed around by someone besides Mom. What if he made me get my elbows off the table or my feet off the couch? School and home, school and home, getting bossed around all day long. I would have to be perfect all the time and that would wear me out.

If Mom spent all her time kissing Mr. Wilson and correcting papers, then when would she find time for me?

I'm glad I get to talk every week with Ms. Montgomery. I told her my feelings because I can't talk to my mom about something that is about her. I can't talk to Eddo either because he's mad at me.

It feels better to talk about feelings with someone instead of keeping them inside, doesn't it? If I don't talk about my problems, I feel like lying on my bed and crying or hitting someone and I don't want to do that anymore.

There's a reason certain words rhyme, like "Sally Jo" and "woe."

January is definitely a depressing month.

Sally Jo's assignment for her future kids:

What is your dream for how you would like the world to be when you grow up? What will you do to make that dream happen?

Who do you talk to about your feelings?

ENTRY TWENTY-THREE, 2/14/84: VALENTINE'S DAY MASSACRE— INTENT TO KILL

February got better, but only for awhile. Do you know that most famines and smallpox outbreaks start in February? February is also famous for a disaster called "Remember the Maine!" when an American warship got blown up in Cuba. Hey, I pay attention during our history lessons! I guess it was just natural, then, that after Valentine's Day we had a disaster in February, too.

We had a big party in our classroom on Valentine's Day. Cindy's mom and Eddo's dad served refreshments. Eddo's dad, who likes to cook better than Eddo's mom does, made sugar cookies in the shape of a heart. He frosted them with pink frosting and stuck heart-shaped red-hots and those little silver things that look like BB's all over them. I want to know how those beebee things are made and how the frosting gets shiny.

Cindy's mom made pink lemonade with red heart-shaped ice cubes bobbing in it. She also brought apple slices to eat to sort of brush our teeth after all that sugar. She is a dietician at the hospital and concerned about those things.

For a game we tried to think of as many songs as we could with the word "love" in them. The winner with nine songs, which was Lisa (who else?), won a big Valentine box full of chocolates. Roger didn't leave her side all afternoon, but not because of love. Well, maybe love of chocolate.

The week before we had drawn names and made our secret person an original valentine. I got Eddo's name. I wanted to write poems like "Roses are red, Violets are blue, A face like yours belongs in a zoo," or "Red is a rose and blue is a violet, Why don't you go soak your head in the toilet?"

Even though those poems are not really mine, but old ones passed down through generations, they are the ones I felt like writing because of Eddo's either avoiding me, or, when he *was* around me, making rude comments concerning Melvin Porter.

Then I remembered what Ms. Montgomery had taught us. She said that if you get hurts and send out hurts again, then the world will be full of hurts. But if you send out goodness when you get hurts, even though it's difficult to do, then the world will fill up with goodness and be a happier place to live in. Because of that, I settled on, "Roses are red, violets are blue/ You are my friend, forever and true."

We made the cards out of construction paper and paper lace. On Eddo's card I drew a picture of his dumb Sherlock Holmes hat and a dog, although I wasn't sure anyone else but me could tell it was a dog. It looked more like a squished piece of licorice with legs. For the final touch, I bought a vanilla candy heart on a stick, punched two holes in the card, and stuck the stick through. When we finished our valentines, we put them in the pouch of the big heart on the wall by Mr. Wilson's desk. After games and refreshments, Mr. Wilson passed out each card.

Roger's card, an orange football pasted on top of a red heart, went to Cindy, and it said, "Hey, Babe, Wanna play ball with me?"

"Sure," Cindy said, and giggled when she read it, probably glad she'd practiced kissing the mirror so much. Lisa gave her dirty looks all afternoon.

Eddo's card was to Shirley, and it said, "Surely, Shirley, you'll be mine." There was no question in Shirley's mind about that. "Oh, Eddo," she squealed, "this is so cute!"

Excuse me while I barf.

My card was from Liz, and it read, "Hey, Baby!" the words above a baby cupid.

"That's sweet, Liz. Thank you," I said.

Eddo opened the one I gave him and then sat there, staring at it.

"Mr. Richards?" Mr. Wilson said.

"Huh? Oh, thank you, Sally Jo." I could tell he said that only because he was supposed to and that he would rather swallow nails.

The rest of the kids got their valentines, but there were two left over.

"What's this? Did I miss people?" Mr. Wilson said. He picked one of the cards and read the name. "Roger, this appears to be another one for you."

"I wonder who sent that?" Cindy asked, and then all the girls giggled, except for Lisa, of course. She tried to look innocent.

Mr. Wilson read the name on the second card. "Sally Jo, here's another one for you."

"Ooooooo!" swarmed all over the room like a runaway ghost. Somebody made kissing sounds.

As Mr. Wilson brought the card over to me, I felt like climbing inside my desk. See, we have these tops that lift up and we put all our stuff inside and most kids don't clean theirs out until the last day of school when they find old bubble gum and used eraser crumbs and papers they forgot to take home to their parents.

Last year Shirley saved all her chewed bubble gum and made a big gumball that was the size of a golf ball by the end of school. She was going to save it for her sister who is one grade behind her to add on to and to enter it in the *Guinness Book of World Records* under the title, "Biggest Gumball Saved By Two Sisters While in the Fifth Grade," or something like that. Instead, the teacher saw it, said it was disgusting, and made her throw it out. That's what you get for having all your hopes of fame wrapped up in a gumball.

All that was going through my mind while Mr. Wilson walked over to me. Who knows why a brain does that and does it so fast? Maybe your brain changes track so that you don't have to feel so embarrassed.

The card he brought me was pink, shaped like a face, and someone had made hair in braids out of red yarn and colored in green eyes and some little brown dots sat on the cheeks. I think it was supposed to look like me.

"Thank you," I said, snatched the card, and shoved it into my desk.

"Aren't you even going to look at it?" Cindy said.

"NO!" I said, and gave her my "CUT IT OUT!" look.

"OK, time for recess. Everybody out!" Mr. Wilson directed, and lucky for me everybody grabbed their coats and took off for the playground. Mr. Wilson always goes to the teachers' lounge during recess to do personal things and to breathe. I know because once I asked him what he did in there and he said he needed a breather.

He left the room before all of us were gone which meant he really needed to breathe today. I lingered, pretending to tie my shoe. When I was alone, I opened my desk and looked at the card. The poem was an acrostic, one that spells a person's name vertically and uses each letter as the beginning for a new line. It said:

> You are:
> Sweet, saucy, smart (You have half my heart!)
> Able, attractive, ambitious,
> Lovely, lively, loquacious,
> Loyal, luminous, and
> Young. A
>
> Jolly journalist, and an
> Outstanding original.
> —A friend

Loquacious? What the heck does that mean? Somebody must've used a thesaurus. I'd have to look that one up. But whoever sent this knew about the heart necklace that besides me, only Eddo and Mom knew about. Maybe Eddo was right. Maybe Melvin did send the necklace.

"Lovely? Loyal? HA!" a voice rang out right by my ear. I whirled around to see Eddo reading over my shoulder.

"What are you doing here?" I yelled. "Lord, you scared me half to death. You shouldn't sneak up on people that way."

"I have as much right to be in this room as you do," he said.

"Well, it's not right to read other people's mail without them knowing or to give them a heart attack."

"I wanted to see what your *boyfriend* sent you." He said "boyfriend" the way you'd say "sewer scum."

"This card and its contents are none of your business," I said, and threw the card back into my desk.

"Why doesn't he just lay off and leave you alone?"

"Look, Eddo, if someone wants to like me, then they have that right. I can't help it, and nothing says that I have to like them back. Besides, I kind of like that card. You sure haven't been saying anything nice to me lately. And I thought you were my friend. That's what I said on the card I made you."

"Well, here's what I think of your card." Eddo ripped the valentine I'd given him in two. "We're not friends anymore. You can be friends with your precious MELVIN." He stomped out of the room.

I just stood there trying to figure out what was going on. One person loved me and one person hated me and I hadn't done anything to make either one of them act that way. I felt like an innocent bystander in the bank robbery of my own life.

"My best friend hates me. My best friend hates me," I repeated to myself as if I could make myself understand by saying it enough times. I felt so lost that the tears gathering at the corners of my eyes turned into sobs and I really couldn't stop them. I ran down to the restroom and into a stall. I flushed the toilet over and over until I quit crying and the bell rang to go back to class.

I didn't even look in Eddo's direction the rest of the day, and after school I heard him say to Roger and some other boys, "Hey, guys, let's go ride bikes, what d'ya say?"

"OK." "Yeah." "Where?"

"How about Sixth Street Hill?" Eddo suggested.

Sixth Street Hill? In February it was wet, slippery, and maybe in this cold weather, icy. Eddo would kill himself. Oh, well, what did I care? He didn't want to be my friend anymore. If he wanted to kill himself, fine with me.

"Gosh, I don't know Eddo. You know it's blocked off to cars. My mom says it's too dangerous in the wintertime," Neal said.

"Yeah, Eddo, same with me," Roger agreed. "Sixth Street is off limits to me, too."

"Well, I'm going anyway. What my parents don't know won't hurt them," Eddo said.

I'd never heard him talk so wild. Melvin Porter was over in the corner, still fooling with his coat.

"Hey, Melvin," Eddo said. "Want to go ride bikes?"

"Huh?" he said, and pushed his glasses back up on his nose.

"Haven't you been listening?" Eddo asked him. "I said do you want to go ride bikes?"

Melvin's face lit up, the big front teeth of his smile taking up half his face. This was probably the first time anyone had asked him to do anything after school. "Sure," he said, beaming. "But I have to leave a note for my dad first."

"Oh, no problem, Melvin. Just say you'll be riding bikes over on Sixth Street. I'm going to go get my dog, so we'll meet you there. It's over by the high school."

"OK. I haven't been there before. I just got my new bike for

Christmas so I haven't been a lot of places yet. But I'll find it," Melvin said, and rushed out.

"Hee-hee," Roger chuckled. "I think it's OK to go over there if I just watch. I have to see this. The class klutz riding a bike down Sixth Street Hill."

"Me, too," Neal said, and they left to leave notes for their parents, pantomiming what they thought Melvin would look like careening down Sixth Street, arms and legs flapping everywhere.

How could he do it? How could Eddo purposely endanger someone's life? He knew that Melvin was not very coordinated. Not even I went down Sixth Street Hill and I could do better wheelies and jumps than Eddo could. He was definitely being the lowest of the low. I didn't care if Eddo killed himself, but I didn't want him killing anyone else. I felt responsible. I had to be there.

———————————

Sally Jo's assignment for her future kids:

Write about a time when you did something stupid or dangerous because you were angry.

ENTRY TWENTY-FOUR, 2/14/84:
THE LIE BACKFIRES

"I'm over at Sixth Street Hill watching Eddo kill Melvin Porter," I wrote in the note I left for Mom on the refrigerator door. I didn't want her to worry that it was ME over there getting killed.

The temperature had dropped by the time I got over to Sixth Street, and the wind blew mist into my face. Eddo and Duke were already there, along with Roger, Neal, and Dave. Duke ran from boy to boy, his tail wagging in excitement because he knew something was up. The guys were joking around so much that they didn't even realize I was there, least of all Eddo.

Melvin arrived on his dorky bike which made the other guys laugh because it was one of those foldable bikes with 8-inch wheels and a tall handlebar instead of a ten-speed like theirs. Another thing that made them laugh was tall, skinny Melvin on his tiny bike looking like Ichabod Crane transported to the twentieth century. I was afraid if he tried to go down Sixth Street Hill, he'd end up looking like the headless bikeman.

"Well, that's quite a bike, Melvin," Eddo said, and I knew he meant the opposite of how it sounded, but Melvin didn't.

"Thanks," he said.

"Yeah, that's really . . . something," Roger said.

"Thanks," Melvin said again. "I'll show you sometime how it folds up. It takes only a minute or two."

"Sure, yeah," Roger said, trying hard not to laugh.

"You ready for a big ride?" Eddo said. He was ready to get on with business.

"OK. Where are we going?" Melvin asked.

"Right down this hill."

Melvin took a look down over the edge of the hill. "Oooh, geez, I don't know. That looks steep."

"No problem," Eddo told him. "It's a piece of cake."

"You go down this?"

"Yep. I do it every day."

I couldn't take this any longer. "You liar, Eddo. You do not!"

"Sally Jo, would you please stay out of my face?" Eddo glared at me. "Who invited you anyway?"

"It's a free country," I said.

"Tell you what, Melvin," he continued, putting his arm around Melvin's shoulder and walking away as if I weren't even there. "Let's toss a coin to see who goes down first. Heads, you go down, tails, I do."

"That sounds good to me," Roger butted in. "I'll toss the coin so you'll know it's fair."

"OK," Melvin said. "I guess if Eddo goes down this hill, then I can too."

"Here we go," Roger said. The coin flew into the air and everyone crowded around to see what came up on the back of his hand.

"Heads!"

That meant Melvin. "Don't do it," I said. "Eddo invited you over here only because . . . "

I couldn't finish. If I told Melvin what Eddo was up to, then that would be betraying a friend, even if he hated me now, and besides, Melvin would think I wanted to be girlfriends with him when I didn't.

"Just don't do it."

"Tombez morte," Eddo said to me. That's a French phrase we saw on a movie once, and it means "drop dead." I couldn't believe that Eddo would say that to me.

"Eddo," I said and even though I said only his name, my eyes were pleading with him to stop this before Melvin got hurt.

"Ready?" Eddo ignored my plea.

"Ready," Melvin said. "Don't worry, Sally Jo. I'll be fine." He turned his bike around and got it headed downward.

"Never fear, the Great Porterini is here!" he said, and took off down the hill.

While everyone watched Melvin's takeoff, I realized why the coin came up heads. Eddo had used the trick coin from his magic tricks kit. Both sides of the coin showed a head. No way had Eddo planned to go down the hill. He had wanted Melvin to go down and wreck.

"You slimeball, Eddo," I said and began beating him on his chest. The other boys whirled around from looking at Melvin to look at me. "You used your trick coin. You knew he'd have to go first. You knew he'd crash and then you wouldn't have to go. You chicken guts!"

Eddo didn't have time to react. Roger pulled me off him before I smashed him to pieces.

"That true?" Roger asked. "Let me see your coin."

"No."

"If you don't let me see the coin, I'll let Sally Jo loose on you again."

"OK, OK. Yeah, it's a trick coin but so what?"

Everyone looked at Eddo but no one spoke. We heard a bunch of yelling down at the bottom of the hill.

"Gosh, we forgot about Melvin," I said. We looked down at him standing at the foot of the hill, waving and jumping up and down. His bike didn't look any more deformed than usual. He hadn't crashed. I felt saved. I didn't have to look at his mangled body and know my friend had caused it.

"Come on back up," I called and motioned to him.

In silence we watched him trudge back up, pushing his bike. As he crested the hill, Roger, Dave, and Neal ran over to him and clapped him on the back.

"Hey, congratulations, man."

"Nice ride."

"Boy, I couldn't have done that."

"Thanks," Melvin said, grinning, and then he looked at Eddo expectantly, waiting for him to say something.

"Yeah, congratulations," Eddo muttered, without even looking at Melvin. He couldn't stand that everyone was on Melvin's side now. Or that everyone knew what he'd tried to do to Melvin.

"Eddo, now it's your turn," I said.

"I need to go home," he said, picking up Duke's leash, and turning to go. "I forgot to leave my mom a note."

"You said you'd go down after I did," Melvin said.

"Are you trying to weasel out of this?" Dave said.

"Chicken, Mr. Two-Heads?" Roger said.

"Scaredy pants?" Neal said.

"Heck, Eddo, you don't need to be afraid," Melvin said. "It's a piece of cake, just like you said."

"Hey, I'm not afraid, all right?" Eddo screeched. His whole plan had backfired. He couldn't stand for Melvin to be the one reassuring him.

"We're waiting," Roger said. "Fair's fair."

"All right. I'm going. I'm going. Hold Duke's leash," he said, giving it to me. At least he was back on my planet.

Eddo situated his bike so it was facing downhill. He took a deep breath and faced skyward. Then he had to wipe off his glasses. The mist had thickened into real raindrops that formed rivulets of water as they joined to rush down Sixth Street. The sky darkened. The heavens grumbled and Duke strained at his leash, growling at the unfriendly noise.

"You don't have to do it," I thought to myself, but I never said it out loud. Now I wish I had.

Sally Jo's assignment for her future kids:
Tell about a time when one of your lies backfired.

ENTRY TWENTY-FIVE, 2/15/84: THE ACCIDENT

*E*ddo went whizzing down Sixth Street Hill, pot-holed, and icy in spots. I didn't realize how cold I was until Duke jumped and pulled at the end of his leash. He wanted to go, too. My hand was so numb I couldn't hold on, and Duke took off after Eddo.

"No, Duke!" I yelled, but the sound drifted with the wind. Duke ran on.

What happened next was in slow motion and all run together, like being on a carousel or when you try to take a picture of a waterfall.

As Eddo reached the bottom of the hill, a car shot out from the street to his left without stopping at the sign, right into Eddo's path. There were two concrete barricades, like dividers between opposing lanes on a highway, across the bottom of Sixth Street to keep cars from coming up, but Eddo's bike went right through the space between them. I guess the driver wasn't looking for anyone to be coming down the hill because of the barricade.

I heard tires screech and Eddo scream and I saw him crank his bike sharply to the right to avoid the car. His front bike tire hit a crack in the street broadside and got wedged in instead of going on over. The bike stopped, but Eddo didn't. He soared over the top of his bike and ended up on the street in a heap, face down several feet in front of his bike.

The car braked to a halt, but not before Duke, following and then passing Eddo, ran right in front of the advancing grill. "Thud," I heard, then a high-pitched "Yip, yip, yip," and then sudden silence.

There they lay, three bodies. Eddo. The mangled bike. Duke.

Nothing moved, not the boys, not me, not the driver in the car, and most horribly, not Duke and not Eddo. Nothing but the wind and the rain. I blinked several times to clear my eyes because I hoped what I had just seen was nothing but a nightmare.

No, it was real. The bodies were still strewn across the street at the bottom of the hill. The driver sat in his car and I could barely see him through the rain-soaked, fogged-up window.

"Sally Jo!" My mother. "I got your note. What do you think you're doing over here when I've told you to never . . . " Her eyes went from me to the bottom of the hill where everyone was looking.

"Oh, my God! Oh, no!" I watched as she screamed and ran on by me down the hill.

The driver, wearing a long, tan trench coat and black driving gloves, got out of his car and stumbled over to the bodies, alternately throwing his gloved hands up to the sky and covering up his eyes. The scene got closer in my eyes, and I realized I'd been running down the hill, too, with the boys close behind me.

"I didn't see them," the man said, first to my mom and then to us. "They were just suddenly in front of me, first the boy and then the dog. I didn't see them. Oh, I feel horrible. The dog just ran out. Did I hit the boy? Did I hit the boy?"

His mouth moved like a guppy's even though his words had run out, and he kept gesturing, like if he moved his hands enough, this would all be gone.

"Please. Pull yourself together and call for an ambulance." Mom grabbed his coat sleeves and held his arms still. He looked at her then. "Please. Hurry," she repeated.

While the man headed for the nearest house, Roger stood over Eddo's demolished bike.

"Don't touch that," I told him. "The police need to see that for evidence." I knew that from watching "Kojak" and "Magnum P.I."

Melvin, Dave, and Neal stared down at Eddo, who was either unconscious or dead, while Mom felt his neck for his pulse, and placed her coat over him.

"Mom?"

"Alive," she said.

My breath exploded in a whoosh. I hadn't even realized I was holding it.

Eddo's right leg lay at an awkward angle and a broken section of shin bone poked through his pants. It was yellow and not white like bones in museums. Yellow, and bloody. His face was bloody, too, and his glasses a smashed mess of fractured glass and twisted metal in the street, along with something else. Stuck right in a crack in the asphalt where he had landed, right in a row in the same order as in his mouth, were his four upper front teeth. When his head bounced back from the impact, his teeth had stayed, ripped right out of his mouth.

I saw the teeth with bloody roots attached to nothing, and I began to laugh. Here Eddo was lying unconscious and I was laughing, but I couldn't stop. The boys looked at me like I was crazy, and Mom shook me, but I kept on laughing. Mom slapped me then, and suddenly, I was sobbing.

"It's my fault, it's my fault," I said, over and over.

"Stop it, Sally Jo, stop it." Mom knelt down, hugged me, and rocked me back and forth as if I were a baby. "This is not your fault."

Little did she know how we'd forced Eddo to ride down the hill when he hadn't wanted to.

"Mrs. Benedict?"

It was Melvin.

"Yes, Melvin?"

"It's the dog, Mrs. Benedict. Duke. He's dead, I think."

I started wailing again. Not Duke, too. If only I'd stopped Eddo, if only I'd grabbed onto his bike and kept him from racing down the hill. If only Duke's leash hadn't slipped through my cold hands. Eddo was hurt, Duke was dead, and over what?

"Shh, shh," Mom said, continuing to hug me. The driver of the car returned and Mom gave him the name and phone number of Eddo's parents and told him to go make another call.

I heard a siren and then saw the ambulance flashing its lights come up the street. The two front doors opened and two men wearing black uniforms ran toward Eddo's body. Another two men appeared from somewhere. They shooed the boys, who had made a circle around Eddo, out of the way.

"Give us some room," one of them said, as they placed a stretcher on the street next to Eddo.

"He has a faint pulse," Mom said, "but he appears to be unconscious. I don't know if he has any more broken bones besides his leg, other than losing his teeth," and she pointed to the teeth still embedded in the asphalt. One of the paramedics picked the teeth up and placed them in a Ziploc bag.

"Your coat, Ma'am?" another one said, and handed it to Mom and she put it back on, blood and all.

"You his mother?"

"No. Neighbor."

He nodded and then the paramedics examined Eddo and put him in a neck brace. While one held the two parts of his leg stable, the others gently placed Eddo on the stretcher and they carried him to the ambulance that way.

"How is he?" Mom asked at the ambulance door.

"We can't give you any information. You might want to check at the hospital or with his parents later."

In the meantime, more sirens and flashing lights signaled the arrival of the police. An officer began interviewing the driver. I watched him gesturing again and the policeman writing in his notebook. Then the driver got in his car and drove away. I covered up my face with my hands and shut my eyes to erase the images. Even in that dark I still saw flashing red and blue lights.

"You a part of this?" asked the police officer, and I realized he was talking to me. The boys were standing in front of him with their heads down.

I nodded.

"I don't know what you kids thought you were doing riding down this hill in winter," the officer said. "What do you think those barricades are for?"

"Cars," I said.

"Don't get smart with me, Missy. They're for bikes too. That means STAY OFF THE STREET! Look what you all caused here today. Do you understand now why this is dangerous?"

Our heads bobbed up and down, even though none of us except for Melvin had actually been riding on the hill. We understood the danger now all too well.

"Don't ride down this hill EVER! I don't want to see you around here again, understand?"

"Yes, sir," various ones of us mumbled.

"Go home. NOW!" The boys shuffled off up the hill, looking back down at the scene every once in awhile. I went to stand by my mother.

The officer spoke with Mom but I don't remember what he said. I was done with listening. When he stopped talking, I turned my head and saw him pick up Duke's limp body and put it in the back seat of the patrol car. The ambulance drove away, and the street was empty again, except for my mom and me.

I felt hard as stone, not even like a person. I was a rock, a frozen lump, standing in the middle of the street in a rainstorm, shivering.

"Let's go to the car, Sally Jo," Mom said, and we trekked back up the hill, through the rain and melting snow. My arms and legs weighed tons, and I walked like a robot. I didn't talk, even when we got to the car in the parking lot at the top.

"I'm going to take us home," Mom said. "We'll call the hospital and check on Eddo's progress."

I didn't say a word.

When we got home, I sat on the couch in front of the wood-stove, and Mom built a fire. Instead of closing the doors of the stove, she put up the screen so we could watch the flames and hear the wood crackling. She left and returned a few minutes later, wrapping the blue, sick-time fleece blanket around me. I saw she wore a blanket around her shoulders too. She'd been all that time without her coat so she must have been freezing too. She had changed into her grey sweats.

"Are you hungry?" she said, but I just looked at her. I wasn't thinking about food.

I heard her in the kitchen, and then she came back in with a bowl of steaming chicken noodle soup.

"Sally Jo, I want you to get some of this down. You got a chill out there, and you're going to get sick if you don't eat some. Please try."

"Mom," I said. "I don't care if I get sick. Eddo is in the hospital and Duke is dead because of me. I'm an awful person. I don't want to eat. I deserve to be sick."

I wept.

"Oh, Honey," she said, and held me close. "You're not an awful person. Tell me what happened. You'll feel better if you talk about it."

"It's a long story. I don't know where to start."

"Just start anywhere. We can fill in the pieces as we go."

"Mom, I made Eddo go down the hill tonight."

"Why do you say that?"

"He tricked Melvin with his two-headed coin so Melvin would go down the hill and wreck. He didn't think he'd have to go down after that. But then Melvin made it and Eddo tried to get out of his part of the agreement, so we called him chicken until he went."

"Eddo has gone down the hill many times before, hasn't he?"

"Yes, but not in bad weather."

"Has he ever crashed before?"

"No, but . . ."

"You didn't know what would happen, did you?"

"No."

"Then you can't be responsible for what did happen. Eddo is responsible for his own actions. You didn't tie him to his bike and force him to ride down the hill at knifepoint. And after all, the whole idea of Sixth Street Hill was his, wasn't it?"

"Yes."

"What I don't understand is why he decided today of all days, in this cold and rainy weather, to ride down the hill."

"That's the long part of the story."

"Let's eat our soup first, then. We both need some warming up."

She went to get her bowl and for awhile, the only sounds were us slurping soup and sucking up noodles.

When we'd finished and set down our bowls on the coffee table next to Mom's tote full of essays to correct, I thought for a moment about where to begin.

"Well, you know about the necklace," I said, and I told her the rest, about the poem and the acrostic Valentine. "Eddo got madder and madder and I don't know why, until today he ripped up the Valentine card I made him and said I wasn't his friend anymore. I kept telling him that I didn't have anything to do with how Melvin feels. Eddo knows I didn't like Melvin's mushy poems."

"Are you sure? Sometimes we don't realize how we feel until someone points it out. After all, you kept the necklace, didn't you?"

"Yes, but that was just 'cause I didn't know who gave it to me."

"But you wore it instead of leaving it in its box."

I had to admit to myself it was nice to have someone pay attention to me like that, someone besides a parent.

"And maybe you began to feel a teensy bit left out when I started going out with Chet, so the necklace made you feel wanted?"

"Maybe. I don't know why I kept it. But I didn't *make* Melvin like me and send me the necklace. Mom, I kept telling him to leave me alone."

"What Eddo saw was someone who *didn't* leave you alone. He was afraid that Melvin would get all your attention. Eddo doesn't realize that love is expandable. The more you love, the more love you have to give. There's not a set quota for love so that if you go over, you have to stop loving someone."

"I'd never stop liking Eddo. He's pretty dumb if he doesn't know that."

"Well, you can tell him that the next time you see him."

Mom and I talked a while longer. She left me alone for awhile, then, to think about things—about friends, love, and disaster and how they were all connected. She called the hospital and asked for Eddo's room. Mrs. Richards answered and we learned Eddo was conscious again, his broken leg was cast, and he was resting. We would be able to visit him the next day.

Later, when she tucked me in bed, I asked her something I'd been thinking about.

"You weren't just talking about Eddo and me earlier tonight when you said people didn't stop loving one person because they started loving another, huh?"

She smiled. "No. I want you to realize that I'll always love your father and you, no matter who else I love."

"Like Chet?"

"Yes. Like Chet."

"OK, Mom."

"Sweet dreams. Sleep tight. I love you."

"Don't let the bedbugs bite. I love you, too."

Now that I had talked everything out with Mom, and Eddo would live, I felt so much better. I could see my best friend tomorrow. I couldn't imagine the rest of my life without Eddo.

I was so tired. I knew I would sleep for days.

But before I fell asleep, I thought about how happy Duke had made Eddo, and vice versa. I cried again. Eddo would be so sad. Whatever would we do about Duke? He and Eddo had been together every day for almost three years. How could Eddo live without him?

Sally Jo's assignment for her future kids:

Write about one of your actions that had a bad outcome even though that wasn't your intention.

ENTRY TWENTY-SIX, 2/16/84:
THE ZOMBIE

The next morning during visiting hours, Mom and I went to the hospital to visit Eddo. Mrs. Richards met us in the visitors' lounge where all the hard, turquoise-upholstered chairs had butt sags from so many waiting people. The walls were all dark turquoise, too. Out-of-date, ripped and mangled magazines were strewn all over the chairs, floors, and one scrawny coffee table stained with coffee cup rings. Crumpled blankets and pillows were stuffed onto one of the chairs.

Mrs. Richards had stayed all night so her clothes were rumpled, her eyes were rimmed red, and her hair uncombed. Eddo's dad had stayed too, but he'd gone home to shower and shave and go to work.

"I don't know how much he'll accomplish at work," Mrs. Richards said. "We're worried sick."

"But I thought Eddo would be all right," Mom said.

"Physically, he appears to be fine, a broken leg and a concussion he's pulled out of. His CAT scan checked out fine. He needs a bridge to replace his teeth. The dentist wasn't able to save them. But that's not what worries me."

"What worries you?" I said. Anything that worried her about Eddo worried me too.

"Oh, Sally Jo," Mrs. Richards said, grabbing my hand and holding on, her chin trembling with the effort of keeping new tears in check. "Eddo won't talk, won't laugh, won't eat, won't do anything but lie on that bed staring up at the ceiling. Losing Duke has greatly affected him. His father and I are at wit's end." With that she began crying all over again.

"Hush, there now. Shh." Mom hugged her like she had hugged me last night. "Of course you're worried sick. And being tired doesn't help. Why don't you go home and get some sleep or at least freshen up? I'll stay here until you get back. Chet's coming over in a little bit to say hi to Eddo."

She patted the tote bag slung off her shoulder, full of student papers.

"I brought my papers because I can correct them here as well as at home. We can manage together."

"Are you sure? Really?"

"Really. Go. Maybe Sally Jo can cheer him up and he'll be fine by the time you get back. I'll call if anything happens."

After Mrs. Richards left, I went in to see Eddo, but I don't think I cheered him up. His bed was over by the window, next to the nightstand with the Kleenex, thermometer, plastic, baby-poop colored water pitcher and kidney-shaped vomit container, and baby powder, stuff hospitals always give you whether you want it or not. The room was totally boring beige and brown with some turquoise and brown pattern on the ugly curtain that surrounded Eddo's bed. The light above Eddo's head was on. Why does that light always have to be on? I remember when I was little and had my tonsils out no one would ever turn out that light, even when I asked. The same antiseptic, hospital-room, stale-air odor clung to my nose.

As his mother had said, Eddo was lying there, staring up.

"Hi, Eddo. How are you?"

He didn't answer or even turn his head to look at me.

"I heard you're going to have a bridge."

No answer.

"Can I drive my car over it?"

No answer.

"Your mom said you had a CAT scan. She said what we all suspected was true. It showed you had nothing in your head."

That was a good joke and Eddo didn't even laugh. Really bad.

"Eddo, come on, you have to talk to me. I'm your friend."

No response.

"I'm going to write 'Eddo loves Shirley' on your cast."

Nothing.

"Can you even see me?" I said, and I stuck my face right in his, looking eyeball to eyeball. He didn't even blink.

I reached out and took his hand, all white and limp, in mine. I held it up to my cheek, like I could suck some of the energy out of me and channel it into him.

"Eddo, I want you to get better," I said.

He still didn't talk. His hand was cold and when I finally laid it down, it hung off the side of the bed until I put it up on his stomach.

Mom came in the room, raising her eyebrows at me in question. I looked at her and shook my head no. She patted me on the shoulder.

"Why don't you go on home?" she whispered. "I'll be there as soon as Nancy returns. Then we'll talk some more. Will you be all right?"

I nodded yes, but my throat clogged up and I couldn't talk.

At home, I felt like doing something but I didn't know what, like when something itches, but you don't know where to scratch. I sat downstairs with my teddy bear Rosco whom I haven't hugged for a year now, and Trixie. Being with Trixie made me think of Duke and then I felt worse.

The doorbell rang and when I opened the door, there stood Melvin Porter, his nose all red from being in the cold.

"Can I come in?"

"Sure." Mom wasn't home but in this case, I didn't think she'd mind. "Go ahead, have a seat." I gestured towards the couch. He sat.

"I came over to see how Eddo is."

"Fine."

"Is he home now?"

"No."

"What's wrong?"

"Nothing."

"If nothing's wrong, then why isn't he home?"

"Quit asking so many questions, Melvin!" I snapped at him. I was about to cry and all he did was ask stupid questions.

"I came over to find out about Eddo. Even though I know Eddo tricked me and I'm plenty mad about that, I feel bad that his dog got killed. I didn't come over to bother you. I guess I upset you anyway. Never mind. I'm going."

He got up and lunged toward the door, then turned.

"Look, I want to apologize for acting so stupid around you this year. It's just . . . you were nice to me when no one else was, not even at home. I mean, my dad is nice, when he's at home, but he's gone a lot with his work, and I miss my mom. I get to see her only at Christmas and on my birthday."

"You don't have a mom?" I hadn't known that about Melvin.

"Yeah, technically. She lives in Portland. My parents got divorced and Dad and I moved here. I didn't know anyone so when you told everyone you'd bop them if they didn't quit picking on me, it felt good and . . . "

He turned back toward the door, still talking.

"I know everyone thinks I'm funny looking. I know they laugh at my clothes. I can't help it though. My dad doesn't have time to buy me new ones and even if he did have time, he doesn't really know how."

Wow. This was a lot of information to take in.

"You aren't all that funny looking. Only a little. But I hated all that mushy stuff you did. Trying to kiss me, and those poems. You coulda just said, 'Thanks for being a friend.'"

"Did you hate the necklace? I saved my allowance for a month to get it for you. A couple of times I didn't eat lunch so I'd have enough money."

Oh, geez. What could I say? Why did I feel like crying again?

"See. Here's the other half." Melvin took the necklace out of his shirt so I could see it—half a heart with a jagged edge as if it had been torn apart. "I never take it off."

I pulled my half of the necklace out from under my sweatshirt.

Melvin's face lit up. "You kept it and wore it," he said, like he'd found the answer to a hard math problem. "You *do* like me." If he'd smiled any more, his lips would have fallen right off the sides of his face.

"Yeah, you're OK, Melvin, but don't get any ideas. You can be a friend, but only a friend, OK?

"Great! The Great Porterini wins again! I'll be the greatest friend ever!" He flopped down on the couch, only he missed and his leg and hip-landed on the floor.

"Ouch!"

"Want a chocolate chip cookie, Melvin?"

"Sure. You betcha." Then pushing his glasses back up his nose, he got serious again.

"I have a confession to make. Where I lived before, there used to be a BMX track and I rode my dirt bike there all the time. I've even won awards in races. When we moved here my dad got me that foldable bike for Christmas because we don't have any room for a real bike in our apartment."

"I suspected you were a good rider because I've watched you go by my house every day. Sometimes you weren't using your hands. So that's why you told me not to worry before you went down the hill?"

"Yeah. Eddo hasn't liked me for a long time, and I felt like he was trying to trick me somehow. I went along with him only because I wanted Roger and the other guys to like me, and you, too. And they do now. And so do you, right? Besides, I wasn't scared. Are you mad?"

"Why should I be? I'm mostly glad you're not in the hospital, too. I'm sorry I bit your head off earlier. I lied. Eddo's not OK. He won't eat or talk and when I told him a great joke, he didn't even laugh. He just lies there in his bed like a zombie. Maybe he doesn't even like me anymore."

"Hmmm." Melvin mused and ate cookies. "That sounds awful."

After his third one, I said, "I have an idea. It might work or it might not. Want to hear it?"

"What is it?"

"Does that mean you want to hear it?"

"Why do you think I asked you what it was?"

"OK. Do you think it would help Eddo to have another dog?"

"I think it's a great idea! When I was a little kid and my dog got hit by a car and died, I cried a lot and drove my parents crazy, so they got me another dog, another puppy. Nothing was the same as my old dog, but the puppy was so cute, I couldn't help playing with it, and pretty soon I forgot so much about my old dog. If it worked with me, it should work with Eddo. Good thinking, Sally Jo! I think you're a genius."

"Oh, Melvin!" I said, hugging him and kissing him on his forehead. "I'll ask Mom, but I'm sure she'll agree it's worth a try."

Then I realized what I had done. Melvin sat there, his mouth hanging open, cookie crumbs stuck to his chin.

"Uhmmm, I think I'd better go." He stood up. "I gotta go ride bikes. Let me know what your mom says. Thanks for the cookies. And thanks for . . . " He pointed to his forehead on his *very* red face, then let himself out the front door.

I was mortified. Why did I do that? I hate that mushy stuff. I kiss Mom and Trixie and that's all. I KISSED MELVIN!! Without even thinking about it. ACK!

I decided to ponder that later. Right at that moment, I hoped Mom would come home soon and we could put Melvin's plan into action.

Maybe, thanks to talking with Melvin, my fortune cookie had been true after all when it read: "You'll know exactly what to do at the right time to get to heart of matters." Just by sitting down and talking, not only would I help Eddo, but my enemy was now my friend.

———————————

Sally Jo's assignment for her future kids:

Sally Jo got her good idea by talking with Melvin. What do you do in order to get your best ideas?

Tell about one time you changed your mind about a person when you learned more information about his or her home life.

ENTRY TWENTY-SEVEN, 2/17/84:
THE PUPPY

Melvin and I tiptoed into Eddo's room the next morning. Except for the light over Eddo's head, the room was dark, so I flicked on the light switch. We crossed our fingers, hoping the puppy idea would work. Eddo's parents and Mom stayed out in the hall. They thought it would be better to let the three of us surprise Eddo alone. Yes, the three of us, because snuggled up warm in a blanket in my arms and trembling the way puppies do, was a Black Labrador wearing a red ribbon around his neck. All shiny and roly-poly, he fit right in the crook of my arm.

Although I was worried about what Eddo would do, I also worried that the puppy might wet on me. Have you ever noticed that baby anythings are usually moist?

Melvin went around to the other side of the bed by the night stand, and I stood on Eddo's left side. He was still staring up at the ceiling like he hadn't even heard or seen us, so I said, "Eddo, we have a surprise for you!" and plopped the puppy right on top of his stomach.

All that weight suddenly dropped on his stomach made air whoosh out of Eddo's mouth, and he groaned, but that was all. He didn't look at us and he didn't talk. Melvin and I looked at each other across Eddo's stomach like, "Oh, no! What if this doesn't work?"

We weren't like magicians who always have another trick up their sleeves. This was our only trick and it *had* to work.

We didn't have to worry for very long, because that puppy had ideas of his own. He wanted to explore this lumpy surface he'd been dumped on, so he got up on all fours and started sniffing his way up towards Eddo's face.

"Pit-pat-pit-pat. Sniff, sniff, sniff. Pit-pat-pit-pat. Sniff, sniff, sniff."

His little tail shook like a windshield wiper. Before long, he reached Eddo's chin which he licked with his tiny, pink tongue.

Maybe Eddo thought his nurse was giving him a strange kind of massage, because he finally lowered his eyes from the ceiling to the puppy.

"Whaaa . . . ?" he said. He didn't have new glasses yet, so I don't think he could tell at first what was going on. He scrunched his forehead and squinted.

When Eddo moved and spoke, the puppy thought that meant he wanted to play and the puppy jumped up and down and barked his cute little puppy bark. "Yark, yark! Yark, yark!"

"Don't piddle on Eddo's middle," I said, and Melvin giggled.

The puppy sniffed and licked again, and by this time Eddo had it figured out. Even if he couldn't see, puppies always smell like puppies, and once it barked, Eddo had to know. His hands moved, grabbed the puppy from both sides around his middle, and placed the puppy's face right in his.

All the puppy kisses he got made him smile, and then he laughed. In the middle of a bunch of puppy barking, Eddo finally looked around his room and noticed Melvin and me.

"Hi, Eddo," I said. "Nice of you to notice *us*. Do you like him?"

I was worried that Eddo still might not talk to us.

Eddo lay back on his pillow, but he kept on petting the puppy.

"Hi, Melbin. Hi, Thawee Jo."

His no-front teeth words sounded funny.

"Do you like him?" I said again.

"Yeah," Eddo said. "Wha-this name?"

"Whatever you want it to be," I said. "He's your dog."

I told him that we knew Duke could never be replaced in his heart, but that Melvin and I had the idea that a puppy could make Eddo feel better about losing his teeth and Duke, and breaking his leg.

"It's like a balance. This will mix a little happy in with the sad. Melvin knew about a puppy who needed adopted."

Eddo looked over at Melvin. I hoped he was thinking how stupid he had been about wanting to make Melvin crash.

"Thanks," Eddo said.

"That's OK." Melvin looked down at his shoes the way he always does.

Then Eddo did something that really surprised me. He held out his hand to Melvin, who finally realized what it was there for, stepped closer to the bed, and shook it.

"Friends?" Eddo said.

"Friends." Melvin beamed. "Gosh, two friends in two days. First Sally Jo and now you." He was almost as excited as the puppy. If Melvin had a tail, I'll bet it would be wagging.

Sitting up in bed, Eddo hugged the puppy to his chest. That reminded me of Shirley and Eddo dancing. The puppy squirmed away so it could breathe the same way Eddo wriggles away from Shirley.

We told Eddo how Mom and his dad had taken us to the pound early that morning to pick out the puppy.

"'Who wants to go live with Eddo Richards?'" we said, and this one came right up to the front of the pen as if he was saying, 'I do! I do!'"

"What are we going to call you?" Eddo said, putting the puppy on its back and scratching its little belly. The puppy nipped at Eddo's fingers.

"How about Duke II? That makes him sound like royalty and that way you'll be reminded of the first Duke too, and all the fun you had together. But it's your choice. That's just my suggestion," I said.

"I like it," Eddo said. "We'll call you Dukie for short, since you are pretty short right now," he said to the puppy.

Dukie barked in agreement and growled, tugging at a corner of the blanket with his teeth. Eddo, Melvin, and I laughed at this puppy pretending to be tough. The sound of everyone laughing made me feel so good, so much better than any Christmas present. Then I noticed Eddo's smile.

"Oh, Eddo!" I gasped. "You look like a vampire."

"Let me bite your neck," he said in a Vincent Price vampire voice, and grabbed my neck and pulled me to him.

I fake-screamed and said, "Quick, Melvin, the garlic!" I made a cross with my fingers, only Eddo didn't bite my neck. Instead, he kissed me right on the mouth and it lasted longer than when your mom kisses you. His lips felt mooshy in the middle without any teeth, but at least he didn't slobber.

"I love you," he said.

You may not think sixth graders say this. To tell you the truth, I didn't think so either but that's what Eddo said, I swear.

The room was silent. Not even my heart beat. I felt myself blushing. I opened my mouth, but I didn't know what to do or say.

"Now you can sing 'All I Want for Christmas is my *Four Front Teeth*,'" Melvin said, saving the day by pretending nothing had happened.

"When the dentist thaw he couldn't thave them, they gabe me my teeth and I plan to put them in a bag with the baby teeth I have left. No way the tooth faiwy is getting thethe. They'll be valuable antiqueth one day, don't you think?" Eddo said.

"Oh, sure." I rolled my eyes. That guy gets some weird ideas, I can tell you.

"I'm going to thave my catht, too."

If he keeps saving things, his bedroom is going to be one heck of a messy museum. Besides, I know from other kids that casts stink after they've been on for awhile and his mom will not allow anything that stinks in his room. Maybe he will keep it up in the treehouse.

A nurse swished into the room and said, "What's all this laughing? Oh, my goodness! A puppy! We can't have this. Animals are not allowed inside the hospital."

I thought her comment was strange because Eddo's parents and my mom had checked downstairs to see if we could bring the puppy in. Because of the special circumstance, we were given the OK. Then I noticed a twinkle in her eye and her big smile.

"That puppy has got to go. If you want to be with that puppy, you'll have to get out of bed and go, too."

"I guess that means we'll have to get you dressed and out of here," Eddo's dad said, as he and Mrs. Richards and Mom came into the room.

"That means Sally Jo, Melvin, and I should clear out then, so you can get ready," Mom said. "Hi, Eddo, good to see you," she added.

"Good to thee you, too, Mitheth Benedict," Eddo said.

Melvin and I said good-bye to Eddo.

"Bye. Thankth for Dukie. Come over thith afternoon, both of you. We can decorate my catht. I'll thow you my old teeth."

"OK."

At the door, Mr. Richards gave us the OK sign and Eddo's mom hugged Melvin and me, saying, "Thanks, both of you for your wonderful idea. I'll never forget it."

Melvin turned red and looked at his shoes again, and I said, "You're welcome."

"Thee you thith afternoon," Eddo said.

"OK," Melvin and I called back over our shoulders, going out the door.

When we got home, Mom said I could take the camera over to the Richards's to take pictures of Eddo with no teeth, and Eddo with Dukie. She whipped up a batch of chocolate chip cookies now that she knew Eddo was alive again, even though she had papers to correct. Melvin and I spent the rest of the morning thinking of stuff we could write on Eddo's cast. We practiced looking excited when Eddo showed us all his teeth.

Sally Jo's assignment for her future kids:

Tell about a time when someone did just the right thing to make you feel better.

ENTRY TWENTY-EIGHT, 2/25/84: WORRIES AND CHANGES

The weekend after he got home from the hospital, Eddo had a doggie funeral for Duke. Besides Melvin (who came with Shirley!) and me, my mom, Mr. Wilson, Uncle Jim, and Eddo's parents, he also invited Roger, Dave, and Neal. Cindy and Lisa were invited too.

We congregated under Eddo's treehouse, standing in a semi-circle facing Eddo. He held a shovel and a paper sack full of stuff. His vampire gap was gone because he was wearing his bridge of brand new front teeth.

Eddo talked about all of Duke's accomplishments like sniffing out Maryanne at the treehouse and he remembered all the funny things Duke did like drinking the punch at our dance. Everyone said what they remembered about Duke. Roger remembered Duke jumping onto the cake at the dance. I told about the first time I saw Duke pulling Eddo into the duck pond.

Then Eddo played "How Much Is That Doggie In The Window?" an old 45-rpm record Mom had from when she was a kid. When Eddo and I were planning the funeral earlier, we didn't think "Amazing Grace" or "Nearer My God To Thee" were good songs for a dog funeral and when we asked Mom if she knew of any good dog songs, she remembered about her record. Mr. Richards strung an orange extension cord out from the kitchen sliding-glass doors and plugged the record player cord into it. Mr. Richards still had his old childhood phonograph that looked like a suitcase with a handle when it was closed up, and he still had a pile of yellow discs to put in the big hole of the record so it would turn on the spindle. I'm glad that our parents saved things from when they were kids because they came in handy.

Since the vet had already disposed of Duke, he wasn't actually there. Anyway, he would've probably stunk bad by then. Eddo couldn't really bury him, but he dug a hole while we all watched. Then one by one, he placed Duke's collar, a peanut butter and salami sandwich, and Eddo's Sherlock Holmes hat and magnifying glass (which really astounded me) into the hole and covered it over. He stuck the little cross he had made from two popsicle sticks glued together in the mound underneath his treehouse.

Next, Uncle Jim played his guitar and sang a song called "Old Blue" about a dog that died.

Some of the words go: "I'm gonna tell you so you'll know, that Old Blue's gone where the good dogs go, singing 'Ya-ho Blue, you good dog you.'"

Because it was a sad song and Duke had been a good old dog, everyone cried, even the boys. I know because I saw them wiping their eyes on their tee-shirt sleeves. It was a good way to cry about Duke and blame it on the song.

Eddo's dad said a prayer for Duke. He kept it short for a change, thank goodness, because I was getting tired of standing there so long.

"Good-bye to our beloved family member. He was full of adventure and good times and we are going to miss him."

"This funeral for Duke is now finished," Eddo said.

The grown-ups went in the house and Mrs. Richards got Dukie out of his crate and brought him out to us.

We took turns playing with Dukie and wrote stuff like "Tough break!" and "2 Sweet 2B 4gotten" on Eddo's cast. Eddo took his bridge out so everyone could see what he looked like without teeth.

"You were so courageous," I told Eddo as I was leaving. "You gave Duke a great send-off and that was hard to do."

We hugged.

"Thank you," Eddo said to my neck.

After Mom tucked me in that night, I started thinking about stuff there in the dark where nothing else intrudes but thoughts. I turned on the light and got out my journal to help me sort out the jumble in my head.

At the start of this school year, I wasn't interested in romance, but I had two boys liking me at the same time. I thought I'd never kiss someone until I was at least 25, but when Eddo kissed me, I felt funny, kind of tingly. I think I'd like to kiss Eddo again and throw my head back like one of those women on the covers of the books Mrs. Richards reads. Eddo hasn't said anything yet about the kiss or what he said after, and neither have I. I wonder what it all means. Maybe the pain pills made him do it. A plethora of things have happened to us since that soggy day in the park when I saved him from drowning in the duck pond and we called each other Vampire Breath and Freak Face. We have had so many adventures together that he is already knit into my life. Are we still friends now or what? Does that kiss change things? If it does, I can think of one good thing. We can still hang out even though his mom doesn't believe in dating because she doesn't know about the kiss.

I think it's great that Melvin showed up with Shirley today. They are both tall and he will be able to breathe when they dance together. Their lips will even be on the same level. I am going to give back the necklace that is the other half to Melvin's heart so he can give it to Shirley. I'm sure that Melvin will agree it belongs around Shirley's neck now.

Mom is probably going to marry Mr. Wilson. He is always here at our house now for dinner and on the weekend, knit into our life for Mom just like Eddo is for me. All that's left now is for him to propose.

I'm not sure how I feel about two teachers in the same house. I worry Mom will ignore me when Chet is around. What if he doesn't like our ways of doing things? What if we don't have waffles on Sunday anymore? What if he says I can't roller skate around the house? What if they make me write essays for punishment every time I mess up?

Or maybe it will be fun to have Chet here to play Scrabble with and go on hikes and watch movies. Maybe there will be some times for just him and me. He's not my dad but I'll bet he will be a good grown-up friend. Maybe he doesn't want to boss me around at all.

In three months, the sixth grade will be over. Three summer months, and then I'll be in the seventh grade. That means figuring out my schedule and changing classes every time the bell rings instead of staying in the same room all day. I will have seven teachers instead of only one. I hope they will be as nice as Mr. Wilson.

Students from every elementary school will be in one giant building and I will only know the ones from my school. I will try my best to make friends with all of them.

Our class went over to look at the junior high and we found out that we'll have lockers to keep our stuff in. I'm worried that I might forget my combination and be late to class. Instead of recess, we'll have P.E. and someone might steal my clothes while I'm out playing.

I suppose I'll have to wear dresses more often. I know I need a new dress right now because my chest is starting to grow. Yuck! When I pass a mirror and look, I am surprised. I see somebody who isn't even me, like a tadpole looking in the mirror and seeing a frog.

So many changes and new things to worry about. I don't have time to worry about the things that happened in the past. Maybe, too, I need to stop worrying about everything that might happen in life. Judging from this year so far, dealing with things as they happen is all I have time for.

What I have learned this year, the main message I understand from writing in my journal is this: Just when you are sure you have all your problems figured out, you get more. Life changes all the time, so you never can count on anything staying the same. I didn't know that when I was a kid. Now I feel more grown up. Not as old as a teen-ager, of course, but older than a kid.

I'm glad I have my journal to write in. It's different from talking to Mom or Eddo, especially when sometimes I want to talk *about* them. And Ms. Montgomery won't be at junior high, so I won't have her to talk to. But I can always take my journal everywhere and write in it. I wonder what I will think about this year when I read my journal a long time from now?

Maybe I will say to myself, "Sally Jo, with so many changes, your hand must have got tired from all that writing. Solving mysteries, overcoming jealousy and tragedy, being kissed for the first time by not just one, but two boys. Your life was really action-packed. Just like in a book."

Sally Jo's assignment to her future kids:

What are some things you worry about and some changes you foresee in the coming year?

ACKNOWLEDGMENTS

First and foremost, my eternal thanks to the inspiration for Sally Jo and Eddo: My son, Sean Weeks and his cohorts, Heather Blaser Dillon and Bryan J. Andersen, who provided me with endless hours of entertainment and story fodder. You made me laugh every day.

Words are not enough to thank my wonderfully talented writing group, the Meat Locker Writers, for their suggestions, guidance and encouragement: Judy Allen, who provided me with Love, Light, and technical advice; Phil Blanton, who filled in with the left brain I lack; Sue Griffith, who asked the best questions; and Richard B. Powers, who reinforced plot and character. I learned so much from them all. I extend a big hug to our new member, Joyce Cochran. I hold them all close to my heart and count them as dear friends. They make Tuesday my favorite day of the week.

My appreciation to novelist, poet and teacher Nancy Slavin who helped me refine my fiction skills and who continues to be the guiding spirit for many fledgling writers.

I remain ever grateful to my first writing group who saw Sally Jo and Eddo grow from seeds of possibility into a story: Nan Phillips (who coached so many), Jack Graves, Jackie Shirley, and Glenn Barber.

I would like to recognize the educators who agreed to use the first incarnation of this book and its writing exercises as a test in their classrooms: Mary Pat Eckley, Shannon Rouse, and Vicki Howry. Also librarian Kathy Anderson, and Oklahoma Writing Project Consultant, Patricia Mumford, for reading and editing.

I am further indebted to the former students who read Sally Jo's journal, and to my most recent middle-grades readers and reviewers, Milan Mafinejad and Eliza G. Thank you, Milan, for also answering Sally Jo's questions at the end of every chapter to make your own wonderful journal. That's just what I'd hoped would happen.

In addition, I am much obliged to all my former junior high and high school students who shared their thoughts and lives with me, and to those who still do now they're adults. Everyone should be so lucky.

I'm beholden to Susan Carrigg of Carrigg Photography and Design for employing her magic to create Sally Jo's fabulous book cover.

A multitude of thanks to Lael Telles for her technical wizardry in formatting my manuscript for Kindle.

Thanks to both the Bay City Arts Center and to the Tillamook County Library for providing space for creative efforts of all kinds to bloom.

And finally, thanks to Neal Lemery, for stepping up to fill whatever need I had—cooking, cleaning, technical support—and for showing me how intention leads to action.

ABOUT THE AUTHOR

Karen Keltz is both a former secondary language arts educator of 33 years and freelance journalist. Her work and photography have been published in *Huff/Post 50, USA Today, The Oregonian, The North Coast Squid, The Ruralite, Oregon Coast Magazine, Poésie, Verseweavers, Oregon English* and *English Journal*, among others. She is a recipient of Willamette Writers' Kay Snow awards for poetry (2008), screenwriting (2009), juvenile fiction (2010) and poetry (2012). In 2011, she won a *Glimmer Train* award for new short story writers. Also, she received awards from the Oregon Poetry Association in 2007, 2008, and 2011. In addition, she was a 2012 recipient of an Oregon Writers Colony poetry award. She lives at Happy House Farm with her husband, two cats, and giant gardens full of indefatigable weeds and moles.

Made in the USA
San Bernardino, CA
11 October 2013